THE
HAMBURGER
BOOK

THE HAMBURGER BOOK

All About Hamburgers and Hamburger Cookery

BY LILA PERL

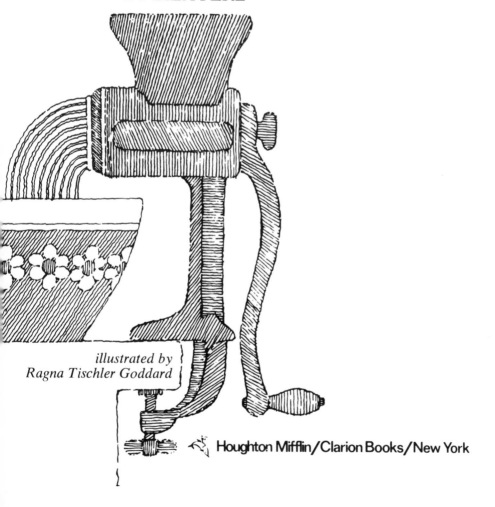

illustrated by
Ragna Tischler Goddard

Houghton Mifflin/Clarion Books/New York

Third Printing

Information supplied by McDonald's
Corporation is gratefully acknowledged.

Text copyright © 1974 by Lila Perl
Illustrations copyright © 1974 by The Seabury
Press

Designed by Ragna Tischler Goddard
Printed in the United States of America

LIBRARY OF CONGRESS CATALOGING
IN PUBLICATION DATA

Perl, Lila.
  The hamburger book.

  SUMMARY: A history of man's use of
ground meat though the centuries, accompanied
by an international selection of twenty-two
recipes.
    1. Cookery (Meat)—Juvenile literature.
[1. Cookery—Meat] 1. Title.
TX749.P47   641.6′6.   73-7131
ISBN 0-395-28921-1

CONTENTS

CONTENTS *(continued)*

RECIPES

ALL ABOUT HAMBURGERS

THE HAMBURGER SUCCESS STORY

What is the one food that you would say is the top favorite in the United States today?

Chances are your first guess would be the hamburger. And you would be right.

Americans eat over 11 billion pounds of hamburger meat a year. With over 200 million people in the United States, that averages out to 55 pounds of hamburger a year for every man, woman, and child in the country.

It includes the 30 to 40 billion hamburgers of the kind you buy at your local or roadside hamburger stand—sizzling rounds of grilled chopped beef, slathered with ketchup, pickle, and onion, and slapped between two halves of a toasted bun.

It also includes those thick, juicy broiled hamburger patties, smothered with stewed or fried onions, the family cook fixes for dinner on Tuesday nights; it includes the sophisticated "chopped sirloin steak" anointed with mushroom sauce and garnished with sprigs of watercress that almost all restaurants feature on their menus; and it includes almost endless variations in the form of beefburgers, as well as numerous other dishes made with chopped, or ground, beef.

The number of dishes—beyond the hamburger patty —that you can create with chopped beef is staggering. There are meat balls and meat loaves, stews and hashes, sauces and soups, stuffings and dumplings, meat pies and all sorts of other baked dishes—just for a start.

The dictionary tells us that hamburger meat is ground *beef*. But we can go a little beyond the standard definition. The first hamburgers, as you will soon learn, were not made of beef. Ground lamb, ground pork, and ground veal make good burger meat, too. In fact, almost any combination of ground meat and/or other ingredients is called a "burger" these days.

There are the familiar cheeseburgers, of course. But there are also pizzaburgers and barbecueburgers, onionburgers and pickleburgers, nutburgers and soybeanburgers. There are also vegetarian "burgers" made with chopped or ground vegetables, nuts, dried peas and

beans, appropriate seasonings—and no meat at all. Totally meatless "hamburgers," admittedly, begin to get pretty far away from the original idea.

Aside from the variety of dishes to which hamburger meat lends itself, one reason it is so popular is that it is quick-cooking—often ready-to-eat in literally seconds. It is also very simple to prepare, not only for a snack or a quick lunch but even when the intended dish is a meat loaf or a chili con carne for a family meal, or a baked *lasagne* or casserole of Swedish meat balls for a company dinner or a party.

Another reason for the popularity of hamburger meat is, of course, its very low cost compared with that of most stewing or potting meat, to say nothing of steaks, chops, and top-quality roasts. But even shopping for hamburger meat takes know-how, and tips for buying it are given in the Hamburger Cookery section of this book.

MAN, THE MEAT-EATER

Meat has been a favorite food of mankind for something like 4 million years. Although archeological findings have revealed that pre-man (a species of advanced ape) existed as early as 14 million years ago, those creatures are believed to have been vegetarian, just as some apes and monkeys are today. Insects were probably the only non-vegetable matter they ate.

Then, in about 4 million B.C., a transition stage began during which the advanced ape began to develop into a composite ape-man. He was not yet a toolmaker, for crude toolmaking skills were probably not developed until about 2 million years ago. But he was learning to kill for his food with rocks, stout tree limbs, or whatever other natural objects lay about him. He was on his way to becoming a habitual meat-eater.

By the time the Old Stone Age had arrived, in about 1 million B.C., primitive man was using roughly chipped stones and crudely fashioned clubs instead of ordinary rocks to kill for his dinner. But since many prehistoric animals were large and fierce, and Old Stone Age man was little more than four feet tall, a favorite method for trapping large animals for food was to cause them to stampede over a cliff or into a bog, through trickery or harassment.

It was probably even more common simply to track sick or dying animals to their final resting place or to eat the flesh, often half-rotten, of those already dead. Of course, there were rats and rabbits and many varieties of smaller game that were easier for primitive man to catch and to slaughter than the giant-size horned sheep or tusked pig of his day.

One thing primitive man surely never tasted was a dinosaur-burger. Even though movies and comic strips have shown us scenes of hand-to-hand combat between a small club-swinging ape-man and an enormous dinosaur, the truth is the two never met! The last dinosaur vanished from the earth 60 million years ago, a good 46 million years before the earliest form of pre-man appeared, and 56 million years before the composite ape-man began to crave meat for his dinner.

Man learned how to create fire during the Old Stone Age, and he may have used it to cook some of his meat. Probably its main use was to char the bones so that they could be cracked open and the marrow sucked out. Heaps of such charred animal bones have been found by archeologists on prehistoric campsites in Asia and Europe. The earliest such campsite known is in the Choukoutien caves near Peking, China, where Peking Man lived, around 400,000 B.C.

The Old Stone Age came to a close in about 8000 B.C. This was followed by the Middle Stone Age (8000 B.C. to 6000 B.C.), during which man began to domesticate animals like the sheep and the goat. He probably accomplished this by selecting and breeding the weaker and less ferocious specimens of the wild forms of these animals. Gradually herds were developed that could be kept on hand as an ever-ready supply of dairy products and, of course, meat.

By the time man got around to domesticating the fearsome aurochs, a great ox that stood seven feet high, had perilously curled horns, and was the ancestor of the world's cattle, it was the year 5000 B.C. and the New Stone Age (6000 B.C. to 3000 B.C.) had dawned. The

wild boar was also developed into the farmyard pig during this period. So, as the master of sheep, goats, and cattle, and a keeper of pigs, man was able at last to turn from hunting to herding, and the stage was set for the first hamburger.

Of course, man never completely gave up hunting wild animals for food. Today the North American big-city dweller often feels the primitive ancestral urge to hunt. He may be an office clerk, shopkeeper, or a corporate executive, but each year he treks to the autumn forestlands on a deer-hunting expedition.

The people of the Old and Middle Stone Ages were not aware of it, but in their day the average person ate more meat than he does today. Of course, the world population was very small then. During the Stone Age, it probably required a span of thousands of years for the number of people on earth to increase from one million to five million.

However, with the development of agriculture, in about 6000 B.C., the earth's population began to take a series of great leaps. While most peoples were still hunters and gatherers, eating berries and nuts, herbs and grasses, roots and shoots, some peoples of the New Stone Age began to plant crops. Herders, in particular, tended to collect close to the major water sources with their animals. There they saw the advantage of growing their own plant food by sowing the seeds of wild grasses.

The Indus River valley in what is now Pakistan, the Tigris-Euphrates valley in what is now Iraq, and the Nile delta in Egypt were some of the sites of early agricultural communities in which wild strains of wheat, barley, and other grains, of legumes and vegetables were developed.

The growth of stable farming communities meant that much more food could be provided than in the past and that many more people could be guaranteed a regular supply of nourishment. Within a few thousand years after the start of this agricultural revolution, the earth's population jumped from about 5 million to reach roughly 250 million at the time of the birth of Christ.

Oddly enough, the increased production of food meant a decrease of meat in the average diet. Agriculture put so many more people on earth that there was no longer as much meat to go around. Meat became a luxury and it has remained a luxury to this day in most parts of the world.

THE "FIRST" HAMBURGER

We have no archeological evidence telling us when the first hamburger was eaten or where. It is almost a certainty, however, that the first hamburgers were eaten raw. Stone Age peoples, having no metal tools, sometimes chose to scrape away at large chunks of raw meat with sharpened, chipped stones. The small particles they collected were easier to chew than gnawing directly on large, tough slabs of raw flesh.

Most people believe that the hamburger, as we know it, was inspired by the Tartars, a Mongol people of central Asia who swept westward in the 13th century A.D. and overran Russia as well as other countries of Europe.

The Tartars were mainly a herding people, wandering with their flocks of sheep across the dry and windy steppes in search of good grazing land. They were also fierce horsemen, who often galloped over the vast, treeless plains of central Asia on raiding missions.

As a people constantly on the move, whether at war or at peace, the Tartars often made a hasty meal from the carcass of a recently slaughtered sheep. Lacking the time to build a fire, it was their custom to prepare a meal by scraping shreds and particles of meat into a mound or patty, for more tender eating. They used their knives for this purpose, but the method and results were not very different from those of their Stone Age ancestors.

The raw "hamburger" meat with which the Tartars gorged themselves was usually lamb or mutton, depending on the age of the sheep that had been slaughtered. The Tartars also ate raw burgers of goat meat, camel meat, and horsemeat at one time or another.

The 13th-century Tartar invaders of Russia were led by Batu Khan, grandson of the terrible Ghengis Khan. The conquerors were known as the Golden Horde, and they established the headquarters of their new empire near what is today the Russian city of Volgograd.

Although the great Batu and the members of the royal court surrounded themselves with luxuries, they and their followers still ate the traditional Tartar foods—fermented mare's milk and raw scraped meat. The Tartar empire held sway in Russia until the 15th century, and the food customs of the Tartars were gradually adopted, with some changes, by Russians all the way from Volgograd, on the lower Volga River, to the shores of the Baltic Sea in the north.

The Russian taste for sour milk and sour cream, which is so important in Russian cookery today, is believed to have come from the Tartar conquerors. But the soured dairy products of the Russian people are prepared from cow's milk rather than mare's milk. The Russians also developed a taste, in the days of the Tartar conquerors, for raw chopped meat. As the Russian version came from beef cattle rather than from sheep, it soon became known as "steak Tartar" or "beef Tartar."

At about the time of the Tartar invasion of Russia, the prosperous medieval towns of Bremen, Lübeck, and Hamburg, in northern Germany, were developing a sea trade. Their ships returned with furs from Russia, amber from the Baltic lands, and fish from Baltic waters. German sea captains also introduced to Hamburg the Russian-Tartar custom of dining on small mounds or patties of freshly chopped raw beef.

To the German *Feinschmecker* (gourmet), the meat had much too bland a flavor. It needed to be seasoned with something more than salt and pepper; it needed side dishes of tangy foods like chopped raw onions, salted anchovies, capers, gherkins, and all sorts of other pickles. Each person could then select the flavorings he liked best. The Germans also liked to enrich their "beef Tartar" by dropping a raw egg yolk into a small depression made in the center of the patty.

Nobody knows exactly when somebody in Hamburg got the idea to cook a serving of beef Tartar before eating it. Perhaps the raw meat had been sitting around a little too long and was no longer as fresh as it should have been. In any case, a thick patty of meat mixed with salt, pepper, finely chopped onion, and a raw egg, somehow got grilled or broiled or fried to a sizzling crustiness on the outside and a tender pale juiciness on the inside. The result was a huge success. The Germans began to call this new delicacy *Deutsches* (German) "beefsteak." To the world at large, it was to be known as "the hamburger."

THE HAMBURGER COMES TO THE U.S.

The hamburger began to travel. During the years from 1830 until the turn of the 20th century, German immigrants poured into the United States in large numbers, driven by hard times, political unrest, and the desire for a better way of life. Today, the population of the United States includes more people of German descent than of any other nationality in the world.

It is not surprising, therefore, that foods of German origin are so popular and so strongly reflected in American eating habits. Hamburgers from Hamburg, frankfurters from Frankfurt, beer, pretzels, potato salad, dill pickles, jelly doughnuts, rye bread, and dozens of other bakery and delicatessen products have all come to America from the land of the hamburger.

The very first hamburger-on-a-bun, however, is believed to have been created in the United States and to have been introduced at the St. Louis World's Fair in 1904. Hamburgers were soon to become a national institution. The hamburger-on-a-bun, like the frankfurter-on-a-roll, was a convenience food that had almost instant appeal to Americans, with their informal, casual, and often hurried eating habits.

During World War I, when anti-German feeling ran high in the United States, the hamburger had to go underground for a while. Sometimes it was referred to as Salisbury steak instead. The name honored Dr. James Salisbury, a 19th-century British nutrition expert who recommended a diet of ground beef and tea as a cure-all for illnesses ranging from gout to tuberculosis. Salisbury steak still pops up on restaurant menus today. It is usually a large thick oval or "steak-shaped" patty of ground beef, broiled or fried, and served with a cooked green vegetable and potatoes on the side.

After World War I, the hamburger's old German-derived name came back into use and the American version, the hamburger-on-a-bun, leaped into the limelight with the opening of the first major hamburger chain, White Castle. This pioneer company, established in 1921, shaped its hamburgers into thin 2½-inch squares and priced them at five cents. To offset the suspicions many Americans had about the purity of ground meat, the chain modeled its stands after the Chicago water tower. The "white" was meant to stand for purity and the "castle" for strength.

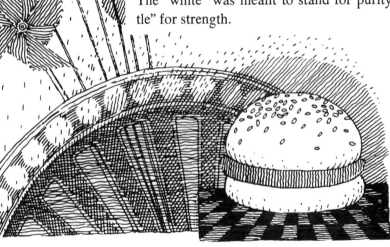

By the 1930's, the hamburger turned up as the favorite food of a comic-strip character, J. Wellington Wimpy, a tearful acquaintance of the famous Popeye the Sailorman, who was himself a ravenous eater of spinach.

While Popeye's spinach caught on almost immediately as a recommended food for young people, it took a little longer for Wimpy's hamburgers to be widely accepted as an appropriate food for children.

There were fairly good reasons for the wary attitudes so many people in the United States had toward the hamburger in the first half of the 20th century.

Even the freshest and best quality ground raw meat spoils quickly because each tiny particle exposes broken tissues and cell juices that are open to contamination by harmful bacteria. The consumer had no way of knowing whether the butcher's grinding apparatus and other equipment were clean and often whether the hamburger meat was freshly ground and properly refrigerated before being sold.

Then, too, some butchers sold ground "beef" that was really a mixture of beef, or of muscle from some other type of animal (pig, sheep, even horse), along with animal parts such as ground tripe (from the stomach lining) or ground snouts and ears. Or the butcher might add a great deal of fat to the meat. Or he might extend the meat by adding cereals, soybean flour, dried milk powder, or other fillers.

People could get around these problems by buying a piece of beef chuck or beef round or sirloin steak at the store, taking it home, and grinding it into hamburger meat themselves. But what about the ready-to-eat hamburger that was sold at the hamburger stand? Perhaps the creator of Popeye and Wimpy was expressing the attitudes of American consumers of the 1930's when he drew Popeye, the spinach-eater, as a symbol of health and vigor, while Wimpy, the hamburger-eater, was fat, saggy, baggy, droopy, and generally unhealthy-looking!

The first Federal Meat Inspection Act was passed in 1906, and the federal pure-food laws of the United States have been setting higher and higher standards for the quality and purity of the foods Americans eat ever since. But without routine inspections, federal control is not fully effective, and states and cities have been adding their own pure-food laws and making investigations on the local level.

Shortly after a 1971 crackdown on careless and dishonest food purveyors in New York City by its Department of Consumer Affairs, a *Consumer Reports* analysis of August 1971 found hamburger-stand products in the metropolitan area to be remarkably high in quality. They were low in fat content, contained pure beef muscle with no fillers or meat by-products, and were well below the limits set for bacterial count.

Supermarket samples of ready-ground hamburger meat from outside New York City did not rate so high in the *Consumer Reports* study. Meat purchased from leading Philadelphia markets showed high intestinal-bacterial counts in 73 per cent of the samples, while meat from three Los Angeles supermarket chains showed insect parts to be present.

Continued vigilance, especially on the part of local authorities, seems destined to remain permanently in the hamburger picture for the future.

THE HAMBURGER GOES ABROAD

After World War II, the food scene in the United States underwent a number of changes. For one thing, the war took millions of Americans out of isolated farming communities, provincial towns, and small cities, and transported them across the world to Europe and Asia. Once the hostilities ended, many stayed on as part of the occupation and peace-keeping forces.

The United States, although it was a nation built by immigrants, had become a melting pot in which foreign cultures often blended and lost their identities. Many Americans were exposed for the first time in their lives to the foods and dining customs of foreign peoples on foreign soil. Food writers are fond of telling us that it was not until after World War II that Americans "came of age" in their new experiencing of international cookery and in their development of more sophisticated tastes in both food and drink.

A reverse situation also took place soon after World War II. The American military personnel who went overseas were followed by American businessmen, American tourists, and American youth gone abroad to study or to serve in the Peace Corps. It was no great surprise that Americans soon introduced their own favorite, the hamburger-on-a-bun, to people of countries all around the world.

In the early 1960's, American companies began to open hamburger snack bars in Paris and London. One popular chain was named Wimpy after the character in the world-renowned Popeye comic-strip.

At first, the French were less receptive to the new idea than the British. In Paris, home of the world's most prideful gourmets, the *om-bour-zhay* was denounced as a food fit only for dogs and other pets. A scientist from the Pasteur Institute theorized that the grinding machines themselves would play host to untold millions of microorganisms and that the resulting hamburgers could not fail to be poisonous.

The hamburger in Paris seemed doomed until it was pointed out that in 1964 Americans were eating nearly 2 billion hamburgers a month at hamburger snack bars in the United States and yet they seemed to be thriving.

It should be noted, however, that since few countries have as much beef as the United States, the American-style hamburger that you are likely to eat in England, France, Italy, Japan, and elsewhere, may contain a high proportion of pork, possibly even some rabbit or horse-meat, plus considerable fat and cereal fillers.

In England, where "Wimpies" were at first quite well liked by most hamburger-addicted British youth, dissatisfaction began to spread in the late 1960's. Wimpy-burgers were criticized by both the British and their American visitors as not being nearly enough like "real American hamburgers." By the early 1970's, new hamburger restaurants like London's Great American Disaster were opening, and "trendy" London youth stood patiently in long queues for the chance to sample, at fairly high prices, what was guaranteed to be "the real thing."

HAMBURGERS
AS BIG BUSINESS

While the American version of the hamburger was reaching new heights of popularity abroad in the 1960's and 1970's, it was becoming big business in the United States. As early as the mid-1950's, "Ma and Pa" hamburger stands and malt shops across the country started giving way to big-name hamburger chains—McDonald's, Burger King, Burger Chef, Hager's, Wetson's, and many more, including the older and expanding White Castle.

Today, in the United States, hamburgers are not just a favorite food, they are a way of life. America lives on wheels. The drive-in movie, the drive-in bank, the drive-in church, the drive-in restaurant are all part of the automotive-convenience picture.

Dinner is easy at the drive-in burger stand. Mom, Dad, and the kids simply pile into the family station wagon. Even the menu is not too long or complicated—hamburger, cheeseburger, or superburger; French fries; a shake or a Coke; coffee or milk; for dessert, ice cream or apple pie. No silverware or dishes are required. All foods are handed across the counter in disposable wrappings and are eaten with the fingers, which, after all, came before forks! The all-purpose automobile quickly converts into a dining room on wheels. Should you bicycle or walk to your nearest hamburger stand, which may or may not have tables or shelves to eat from, you can always eat a hamburger standing up, walking, or even on the run.

The basic variety of hamburger-stand burger ranges in price from about sixteen cents (for the small "Buy 'em by the 'Sack' " White Castle brand) to about thirty cents at some of the other major chains. The meat inside the bun ranges in weight from a little less than one ounce to slightly over an ounce, before cooking. Compared to good-quality bulk hamburger meat that you buy at your supermarket for about $1 per pound, ready-to-eat burgers are expensive—$2 to $3 per pound for the meat. Of course, you get the bun and the relishes, too—and there is no cooking to do before or dishes to wash afterward.

The leading hamburger chains have become big business in the United States because they have learned the art of selling convenience to a servantless and efficiency-

oriented public at what appears to be a reasonably low cost. At the same time, the chains sell confidence, the assurance that, through brand-name standardization and rigidly controlled regional distribution, all their products will be pure, wholesome, and unvarying in taste.

Like many of the motel and hotel chains, shops, and services around the country, most food-dispensing chains are franchise operations. This means that big-name hamburger stands, for the most part, are run by individual owners who buy the chain-name and formula under a licensing agreement and in keeping with a strict set of rules. This combination of a private business operator selling a uniform product or service under the coast-to-coast umbrella of a big-name chain enterprise seems to work very well.

McDonald's, among the largest of the food franchisers, with twenty-two hundred shops in the United States (including Alaska and Hawaii) and Canada, and rapidly expanding into Germany, Holland, Japan, Australia, Latin America, and the Caribbean, is proud to tell you that the McDonald's hamburger you eat in Boston will taste precisely like the one you eat in New Orleans or Milwaukee, in San Francisco or Albuquerque. McDonald's makes sure of this. Each of its shops uses the same kind of pure beef, with a fixed percentage of fat, which is shipped or delivered to it from a controlled regional source.

Every pre-shaped (basic type) hamburger that is stacked in the refrigerator or freezer locker of a McDonald's shop is .221 inches thick, 3.875 inches in diameter, and weighs 1.6 ounces. Buns, pickle slices, ketchup, dehydrated onions, French fries, and shakes are all standard and unvarying also. The same is true for the fried fish-filet sandwiches that McDonald's added to its menu in 1964, the apple pie added in 1967, and the "Big Mac" added in 1968. All store managers and owner-licensees are graduates of McDonald's Hamburger University in Elk Grove, Illinois, where a quick course in management training earns them the degree of "Bachelor of Hamburgerology."

The "kitchen" of the modern hamburger stand is really an assembly line where the hamburgers are grilled, the split buns are toasted, the relishes are dabbed on, and the disposable packaging is added. The "chefs" range from part-timers, mostly high school and college students, to experienced short-order cooks and countermen. But all have similar jobs, mainly responding to the buzzers, bells, clicks, and other timing-device signals that tell them when the food is done and ready for the next step, which is usually the counter chute, followed quickly by the customer. At McDonald's the assembly-line hamburger takes a maximum of 55 seconds to put together. If it is not sold in 10 minutes, it is thrown away.

Despite guarantees of freshness and purity, the typical hamburger-stand meal of burger, fries, and shake leaves much to be desired from a nutrition standpoint. It is high in calories and in saturated fats, which are believed to raise the body's cholesterol count, and it is low in vitamins B and C and in protein, very little of which is supplied in a burger ranging from under one ounce to about an ounce-and-a-half, before cooking.

The success of the big-business hamburger chains also seems to tell us something disappointing about life in the United States today. Perhaps the assembly-line hamburger is the price America must pay for its rapid growth as an industrial nation and a world power, for the ambitious hard-working character of its people, for its worship of speed, efficiency, and convenience.

Yet it does seem contrary that in a land brimming with the natural wealth of its farms, its orchards, and its grazing lands, its rivers, lakes, and oceans, in an economy excelling in food-processing and marketing know-how, in a nation rich with the heritage of immigrant peoples from every corner of the globe, that so many Americans should turn their backs on so much variety and appear content with the uninspired, mass-produced, fast-food hamburger.

Hamburger meat itself is one of America's and the world's most versatile foods. In the United States alone, there are rich regional traditions for dishes other than hamburger patties that are prepared with chopped or ground fresh beef. New Englanders put chopped or finely-diced beef into creamed dishes and gravy-brimming potpies, while at the opposite end of the country, in the Southwest, chili dishes that combine hamburger meat and red beans in a spicy sauce are everyday fare. And all across the United States, meat loaves and meat balls (served in stews, sauces, and soups; with pasta and with vegetables) are great family favorites.

European, African, and Asian peoples have been even more imaginative in their use of hamburger meat. Their recipes are today influencing American tastes more and more, partly because many of us are becoming tired of steak-and-potatoes eating (or hamburger-and-French fries, as the case may be) and are searching for variety; partly because of the high cost of meat and the world's shrinking meat supply.

American families are learning that the "poverty" dishes developed by foreign peoples around the world are wonderfully budget-slashing as well as being remarkably appetite-teasing. When such specialties as a Brazilian meat hash, an Italian meat sauce, an Indian ground-beef curry, or a Mexican tamale dish are combined with rice, pasta, corn, or a dough product, a pound of hamburger can be extended to serve six to eight people rather than the three or four people it would serve if it were simply shaped into quarter-pound hamburgers and grilled.

The wide world of the hamburger, with its economical but nutritious, exotic but easy-to-prepare, dishes awaits your exploration in the section that follows: Hamburger Cookery Around the World.

HAMBURGER
COOKERY
AROUND THE
WORLD

THE WORLD'S SHRINKING MEAT SUPPLY

Today there are 3.7 billion people on earth; in the year 2000 there will probably be 7 billion. Each year there is less meat per person available, simply because the world's meat supply cannot keep pace with its rapidly growing population. In the pre-agricultural era, at a time when there were perhaps only 5 million people in the world, meat was a plentiful, everyday food. Today it is a luxury food for most.

If the total amount of meat produced in the world at the present time was equally distributed, each person would receive about 40 pounds per year, or 4/5 pound per week.

Most people in the United States would be very discontented with only a little over twelve ounces of meat a week. But millions of people in Asia, Africa, and Latin America would be overjoyed with such a bonanza of well-liked protein food.

As it is, the world's meat supply is very unevenly distributed, not only between countries but also *within* countries, particularly in Latin America. In the United

States, each person now eats an average of about 192 pounds of meat a year. According to recent figures, average per capita meat consumption is even higher in the meat-producing countries of Argentina (198 pounds), Uruguay (213 pounds), Australia (215 pounds), and New Zealand (233 pounds).

On the other hand, the overwhelming majority of the world's peoples, particularly those in the "hunger areas," sees little or no meat from one year's beginning to another year's end. They eat monotonous diets, as poor people do everywhere, of predominantly carbohydrate foods: rice in Asia, corn in Latin America, cassava, millet, and sorghum in Africa.

Unlike meat, eggs, milk, and fish, most hunger-area foods are not only low in protein, but supply a poorer quality of protein than do foods from animal sources. Vegetarians point out that some vegetable proteins, such as those found in soybeans and chickpeas, are almost as good as the proteins found in meat. But, in practice, it is very difficult to persuade a habitually rice-eating or corn-eating people to accept an unfamiliar agricultural food, even with the assurance that it is more protein-rich than the food on which they normally subsist. Meat, on the other hand, is almost always welcomed by protein-hungry people.

India is a troubling exception here. With more cattle than any other country on earth—about 176.5 million head—Indians suffer severely from hunger and malnutrition, partly due to the Hindu religious taboo that forbids the killing of cattle, which are regarded as sacred.

Nutritionally, meat is a very superior food because its "complete" protein supplies all of the essential amino acids, chemical organic compounds that the body cannot manufacture but must get directly from food, completely formed and ready for use. Protein malnutrition and protein hunger, whether due to lack of animal proteins or of high-quality vegetable proteins, cause serious deficiency diseases and also mental retardation. It is estimated that 300 million children growing up in the developing countries of the world will be retarded. It is also estimated that one-third of the world is hungry and that 10,000 people die each day due to hunger and malnutrition.

With protein foods of animal origin in such short supply and so time-consuming and costly to produce, the eventual doubling of world population will probably result in large-scale protein starvation for mankind.

The meat that is available in the world today comes from a variety of animals. Although animal flavors differ, the quality of protein contained in meat muscle is about the same. Half of the world's meat supply now comes from beef cattle; about 40 per cent from hogs; and 8 per cent from sheep and goats. The remaining 2 per cent comes from buffalo, camels, horses, reindeer, rabbits, kangaroos, deer, antelope, and other game animals.

Way back in the Stone Age, man began to develop ways of storing some of his food supply. Drying, salting, smoking, and other means of preservation made it possible to space out the fruits of a harvest, a catch, or a kill, instead of eating on the spot whatever came to hand. As civilizations developed around the world, people began to establish regular dining patterns and learned to combine the elements of their daily diets, even when very limited, into remarkably tasty and appealing dishes.

In countries or regions of the world where meat was

scarce, it became common practice—and common sense
—to stretch the supply by cutting the meat into very
small pieces, scraping away all the scraps and shreds that
clung to the bones, and combining such bits and pieces
with vegetables, grains, and other more plentiful foods.
Stews have always been popular among meat-poor people around the world. But hamburger is, without a doubt,
the most stretchable of all meats.

The recipes that follow show how hamburger and
other ground meats (mainly lamb and pork) are used
in the cookery of lands where meat is both plentiful and
not-so-plentiful.

Many of these recipes clearly demonstrate how necessity has created some of the most inspired dishes in international cuisine. Most are basically stews, hashes, or
casserole bakes, in which relatively modest amounts of
meat are used for the number of portions served: *lasagne*
from Italy; *moussaka* from Greece and Turkey; chopped
steak and bananas from Tanzania; sweet-and-pungent
pork balls from China; *picadinho* from Brazil; and *chili
con carne* from the southwestern United States.

From countries where more meat is available, such as
those of northern Europe, there are recipes for thick
Russian meat cakes and German burger steaks. And from
the United States, there are recipes for regional ground-
beef dishes of the American past as well as for favorite
home-cooked American-style burgers of the present.

HOW TO BUY AND STORE HAMBURGER

Before trying any of the recipes in this book, you will need to buy the hamburger. Since no recipe is any better than the sum of its ingredients, here are some tips to help you select the best possible meat for the dish you are going to prepare.

Most meat counters offer two or three different grades of hamburger for sale. All are ground beef unless otherwise stated, but they vary as to the amount of beef fat that has been ground with the meat.

According to the standard set by the United States Department of Agriculture, hamburger meat may not contain more than 30 per cent fat. The cheapest grade of hamburger, sometimes labeled "regular ground beef" or simply "hamburger," usually contains 20 to 25 per cent. This is too much fat to make a satisfactory cooked hamburger dish. As the meat cooks, it shrinks to three-quarters or less of its original bulk and the fat oozes out into the pan. In making a chili or a stew, the cooked dish will be greasy. Although it may be priced very low, hamburger meat with high fat content is not a good buy.

Middle-priced hamburger is sometimes labeled "ground chuck" and contains 10 to 20 per cent fat. The highest-priced ready-ground hamburger is usually labeled "ground round" and contains less than 10 per cent fat.

Middle-grade hamburger is generally a good buy, provided there are not too many white particles of fat mixed with the meat. Compare its appearance to that of the higher-priced, leaner hamburger. A little fat is desirable as it improves flavor. If, however, middle-grade hamburger looks somewhat high in fat content, it is a good idea to buy an equal amount of lean hamburger and mix the two together.

All packaged hamburger meat should have been freshly ground, or if you prefer you may have the hamburger meat of your choice ground to order. Packaged hamburger should not look dark or dried-out or brown at the edges.

As a general rule, one pound of hamburger meat serves four. But this can vary depending on what other ingredients are mixed with the meat or added to the dish, what accompanying dishes are served, and, quite simply, what size appetites are involved.

Always store hamburger in the refrigerator in a covered bowl, and try to use it the same day you buy it or the very next day at the latest.

Raw hamburger meat freezes well and may be kept two to three months in a freezer that stays at 0 degrees Fahrenheit. Before wrapping the hamburger meat in freezer paper (preferably aluminum foil), shape it so that it is no more than one inch thick; then it will freeze quickly.

It is a good idea to divide each pound of hamburger

into half-pound or quarter-pound portions before freezing. Wrap each portion in a separate piece of wax paper within the freezer wrapping. Be sure to label each package. Hamburger meat can also be shaped into patties before freezing. Very thin patties can be cooked without defrosting.

Ready-frozen raw hamburger patties, sold under commercial brand-names in many supermarkets and food stores, are generally not a good buy. Of several samples tested in the *Consumer Reports* study of August 1971, only about 5 per cent rated as "good." Most were tough and rubbery and contained gristle and bone chips. The cost of the commercially frozen patties averaged 60 per cent higher than the supermarket price of fresh bulk hamburger meat. Also, there was the danger that this highly perishable product had not been consistently kept at proper freezing temperatures during its store life.

A hamburger-related product has recently appeared on supermarket shelves. Known under various brand names as Hamburger Helper, Hamburger Skillet Dinner, etc., the 7- or 8-ounce cartons contain such ingredients as rice, noodles, macaroni, dehydrated potatoes and other vegetables, seasonings, thickeners, and artificial flavorings and preservatives. Combined with water and a pound of hamburger meat, they provide quick chili, hash, Stroganoff, Romanoff, and oriental-type main dishes, depending on the variety chosen, and feed four or five people. Although convenient and generally satisfying to the palate, the cost of "help" for hamburger meat comes high when using these products. At close to sixty cents a box, the unit price runs from $1.15 to about $1.30 per pound, as much as or more than the price of the hamburger!

Much better value in terms of both cost and nutrition (and of course providing much greater variety) is obtained when preparing hamburger dishes "from scratch" or with only some "convenience" ingredients in the recipe to speed things along.

When a recipe in this book calls for hamburger, it always means ground beef. If the recipe calls for ground lamb or some other ground meat, it will specify what meat.

HAMBURGER COOKERY IN EUROPE

GERMANY Long before the 20th-century invasion of the American-style hamburger, Europeans were cooking dishes made with hamburger meat. After all, Germany gave the world the original hamburger, its *Deutsches* "Beefsteak."

Germans are dumpling-lovers, too, and while they cook numerous kinds of dumplings made of flour, bread, or potatoes, they have also devised a meat dumpling, a plum-sized meat ball simmered in beef stock and served with a sauce of capers (pickled flower buds). Interestingly enough, *Königsberger Klopse,* as these meat dumplings are called, contain eggs, onions, and anchovies, so you can see how the originally raw dish, beef Tartar, developed into more than one kind of cooked hamburger dish in German hands.

While poorer nations tend to extend their meats by combining them with starchy foods or vegetables, Germany shows its prosperity, its taste for rich eating, and the natural wealth of its coast and farmlands by serving meat-and-fish and meat-and-egg combinations. Austrians, too, like to top a fried veal cutlet with a garnish of anchovies or with a fried egg. In fact, the American inclination for ham-and-eggs, bacon-and-eggs, and hash-and-eggs is distinctly due to German influence.

Here is the recipe for Germany's first cooked hamburger, a thick, hearty oval patty containing over a quarter of a pound of meat—and of course an egg.

DEUTSCHES "BEEFSTEAK" (Germany)

1 ¼ *pounds hamburger*
1 *egg, beaten*
2 *teaspoons grated raw onion or dried chopped onion*
2 *teaspoons finely-cut fresh or dried parsley*
¾ *teaspoon salt*
  pinch white pepper
2 *tablespoons flour*
2 *tablespoons butter*
  flour to coat hamburgers

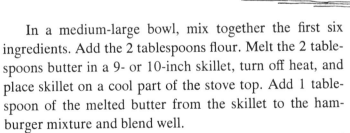

In a medium-large bowl, mix together the first six ingredients. Add the 2 tablespoons flour. Melt the 2 tablespoons butter in a 9- or 10-inch skillet, turn off heat, and place skillet on a cool part of the stove top. Add 1 tablespoon of the melted butter from the skillet to the hamburger mixture and blend well.

Divide hamburger mixture into four equal parts and shape each into a large, thick, oval patty. Coat each on one side *only* with flour.

Place skillet over medium-high heat and bring the remaining butter in the pan to sizzling. Place the 4 hamburgers in the pan, floured side down. Fry, uncovered, until crusty-brown on bottom. Turn hamburgers. Lower heat to medium-low and fry about 5 minutes, uncovered.

Place cover on skillet, leaving it slightly to one side, so that cooking steam can escape and hamburgers will not become soggy. Continue frying on low heat for 10 to 20 minutes, depending on whether the hamburgers are preferred rare, medium, or well done on the inside. Serve at once.

Makes 4 servings. MENU SUGGESTION: serve DEUTSCHES "BEEFSTEAK" with home-fried potatoes with bits of fried onion in them and with buttered green peas.

SCANDINAVIA In the Scandinavian countries of Sweden, Norway, Denmark, and Finland, fish is such an important item in the diet that it stands alone. But dairy production (particularly of cheese) is very high, so it is not surprising that *köttbullar,* the famous Swedish meat balls, are fried in butter and are often cooked in a sauce containing milk or cream. In Denmark, these meat balls are called *frikadeller*. Norwegians call their meat balls *kjott boller*. Ground pork and/or veal is usually mixed with the beef. Scandinavians use a variety of spices in their cookery, a result of their sea trade with the spice-rich lands of the East. Cardamoms, anise, saffron, ginger, allspice, and nutmeg go into baked goods and desserts. The last two often turn up in meat balls as well!

Köttbullar have their place on the famous Swedish *Smörgåsbord*, which translates as "butter and bread table" but is really a groaning board of appetizers, snacks, salads, hot dishes, and cheeses, at which guests help themselves. The foods are eaten in strict order at one of these Viking-style feasts. Herrings and shellfish come first to whet the appetite. Cold meats, salads, and relishes are next, followed by meat balls, meat-stuffed cabbage rolls, fish balls in cream, baked brown beans, and other zesty hot dishes. Lastly come cheeses, dessert, and coffee.

While not all Scandinavians eat this well, and certainly not all the time, the food bounty of the affluent countries of northern Europe is well demonstrated at the Swedish *Smörgåsbord*, the Danish *Smorrebrod*, and the Norwegian *Koldtbord*.

KÖTTBULLAR (Sweden)

¼ pound lean ground pork plus ¾ pound hamburger, or 1 pound hamburger
1 cup finely crumbled whole-wheat bread (about 2 slices)

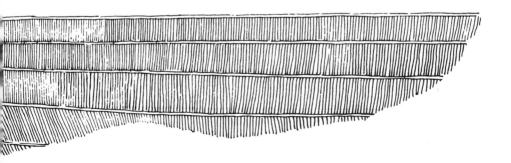

¼ *cup milk*
2 *teaspoons grated raw onion or dried chopped onion*
¼ *teaspoon ground nutmeg*
1 *egg, beaten*
¾ *teaspoon salt*
flour to coat meat balls
1 ½ *tablespoons butter*
1 *cup hot water*
2 *beef bouillon cubes*
½ *cup milk or light cream*
2 ½ *tablespoons flour*
2 *teaspoons finely-cut fresh or dried parsley*

Combine first seven ingredients. Form meat mixture into small balls, one inch in diameter (about 42). Coat balls lightly with flour.

Melt butter in a deep 9- or 10-inch skillet over medium-high heat. Add meat balls and brown on all sides. Lower heat to medium-low. Remove meat balls with a slotted spoon and set aside in a bowl.

Spoon off excess fat from skillet. Add hot water and beef bouillon cubes. Stir with wooden spoon until cubes have dissolved, combining pan scrapings with liquid.

To milk in measuring cup, add flour and stir until perfectly smooth. Pour into skillet and cook, stirring, over medium heat until sauce has thickened. Add meat balls, sprinkle with parsley, and heat through gently.

Makes 4 to 6 servings. MENU SUGGESTION: serve KÖTTBULLAR with buttered broad noodles and hot beets, sweet-and-sour style.

RUSSIA   The Soviet Union, with the third largest cattle population in the world, after India and the United States (nearly 90 million animals), eats a far more evenly distributed meat diet today than in czarist times. The Russians, who, after all, learned about chopped meat from the Tartars, have all sorts of cooked ground-beef patties in their cuisine. These go by a variety of names depending on size and shape. *Kotletki* are smaller than *kotleti,* and *bitochki* are tinier than *bitki.* Russians are fond of diminutive and pet names. *Golubtsi* ("pigeons") are plump cabbage rolls stuffed with chopped meat and rice. They originated in the Ukraine. *Luli kebab,* a chopped-lamb patty, comes from the sheep-raising regions of southern Russia.

Ever since the Tartars introduced the idea of soured milk, the Russians have been putting sour cream into soups, on top of pancakes, and into meat dishes like *beef Stroganoff,* so of course the Russian hamburger cakes known as *bitki* are smothered in a sour cream-and-mushroom sauce.

BITKI (Russia)

1 cup *finely-crumbled day-old white bread (about 2 slices)*
¼ *cup water*
¾ *pound hamburger*
1 *tablespoon dried chopped onion*
½ *teaspoon salt*
⅛ *teaspoon black pepper*

   2 tablespoons sour cream
     flour to coat meat cakes
   1 tablespoon butter or margarine
   ¾ cup condensed cream-of-mushroom soup
   ⅓ cup sour cream
    1 teaspoon lemon juice
    1 teaspoon finely-cut fresh or dried parsley

Put crumbled white bread into a medium-large mixing bowl. Sprinkle water over bread and toss lightly to moisten evenly. Add hamburger, onion, salt, black pepper, and the 2 tablespoons of sour cream. Mix well.

Shape hamburger mixture into 2-inch balls and flatten them slightly. You will have about 12 small cakes. Roll meat cakes in flour to coat lightly.

Melt butter or margarine in a deep 9- or 10-inch skillet over medium-high heat. Add meat cakes and brown well on both sides, turning them with a spatula. Turn off heat and place skillet on a cool part of the stove top. Remove meat cakes to a plate. Spoon off any excess fat from skillet.

In a small mixing bowl, combine the condensed cream-of-mushroom soup (as it comes from can; do not dilute), the ⅓ cup sour cream, and the lemon juice. Pour this mixture into the cooled skillet and, using a wooden spoon, blend it with the pan scrapings. Add meat cakes. Sprinkle with parsley. Cover skillet and heat through gently on low heat. Do not boil.

Makes 3 to 4 servings. MENU SUGGESTION: serve BITKI with kasha (buckwheat groats) or brown rice and a cucumber salad.

GREAT BRITAIN The English were at one time regarded as the staunchest meat-eaters in all of Europe. Today the wild boar, the venison animals, the hares, the pigeons, and the game birds are much depleted, and grazing lands for meat animals are so greatly reduced that England is now the world's largest importer of meat —beef from Argentina, lamb from Australia and New Zealand, ham and other pork products from Denmark.

The British, however, have always appreciated "minced," or chopped, meat of various kinds and have most often combined it with extenders such as piecrusts, pastries, batter doughs, and cereals. However, such specialties have not traveled very far. Perhaps this has something to do with their ingredients and the peculiarly British names by which they are known: *black pudding* (pork sausage, pig's blood, suet, and oatmeal); *toad-in-the-hole* (sausage or other minced meat baked in a batter similar to that of Yorkshire pudding); *haggis,* the famous Scots dish (grated sheep's lungs, heart, and liver mixed with suet and oatmeal, stuffed into a sheep's stomach and boiled).

Cornish pasties (chopped lamb or beef, diced potatoes, and onions baked in a pastry turnover) have done somewhat better. Originally the lunch food of tin miners in Cornwall, the pasties (pronounced pass'-teez) traveled to Wisconsin with a large contingent of emigrating Cornishmen. *Pork pies* and *sausage rolls* (crumbled sausage meat in a "blanket" of flaky pastry dough) are well liked abroad by Australians and New Zealanders. For the Englishman on his native soil, *sausage and chips* (fried potatoes) are the closest thing to the American hamburger and French fries, unless of course he has already gone

"Wimpy" and is eating American at home.

Lamb and mutton, whether raised in the British Isles or imported from the Commonwealth countries of New Zealand and Australia, are British favorites when it comes to chops and roasts. The British eat about 20 pounds of lamb and mutton per person per year (Americans eat 4 pounds; Frenchmen eat 7). Lamb-burgers are sometimes served, instead of a lamb chop, along with a slice of lamb liver, a lamb kidney, a slab of black pudding, and a grilled tomato, as part of an *English mixed grill.*

LAMB-BURGERS WITH BACON (England)

    8 strips lean bacon
 1 ½ pounds lean ground lamb
    1 teaspoon salt
   ¼ teaspoon white pepper
   ¼ teaspoon dried parsley or dried marjoram
    1 teaspoon lemon juice

Place bacon strips in a cold 10-inch skillet. Fry bacon over medium heat until crisp and brown on both sides. Spoon off bacon fat from skillet as it collects, placing it in a small bowl to solidify before being thrown away. Lift cooked bacon out of skillet with a slotted spoon and place it on paper toweling to drain fat. Let skillet cool.

In a large mixing bowl combine remaining ingredients. Shape into four large patties about one inch thick.

Heat 2 tablespoons of the bacon fat in the skillet over medium heat. Add lamb patties. Cook until brown and crusty on bottom. Turn with spatula. Brown on other side. Then reduce heat to low, place cover on skillet slightly to one side to allow steam to escape, and continue cooking on low heat for about 15 minutes, spooning off any additional fat that accumulates. Cooked lamb-burgers should be juicy and faintly pink in center.

Uncover skillet, add bacon strips just to crisp and heat. Serve lamb-burgers at once, each garnished with 2 strips of bacon.

Makes 4 servings. MENU SUGGESTION: serve LAMB-BURGERS WITH BACON with shoestring French-fried potatoes and grilled tomato halves.

FRANCE   French cuisine has been rather restricted in its use of *boeuf haché* (chopped beef). Most often French hamburgers are prepared by mixing the meat with red wine and cream, and then simmering them in a sauce of burgundy wine. One reason for the general aversion to chopped-meat dishes in France is the rather widespread sale of horsemeat in that country. While few peoples since the Tartars have cared for horsemeat—and most Europeans and Americans regard it with horror as a food for humans—Paris has had horsemeat butcher shops for centuries.

Horse steaks from young animals are rated very high by those French who accept horseflesh. However, as most of it comes from aging work animals, it is usually tough and is purchased ground. By French law, the horsemeat butcher must grind the meat in the customer's presence. Some Parisians eat their horseburger meat raw, a true "steak Tartar." Others mix it with chopped beef, pork, or veal, and cook it. The French are estimated to eat about as much horsemeat per person per year as Americans do lamb—roughly 4 pounds.

In general, the French seem to prefer to stretch their meat supply through the use of stews rather than hamburger dishes. Bits of rabbit or lamb or animal parts such as kidneys, brains, oxtails, and tripe, are cooked with vegetables and sometimes with dried legumes. The French also eat many kinds of *charcuterie* (sausages), which are sold in special pork-butcher shops.

SPAIN AND PORTUGAL   Louis XIV, France's famous "Sun King," stated in the late 1600's, "Europe ends at the Pyrenees." Perhaps he meant by this that Spain and Portugal, the two countries of the Iberian peninsula, were very different in their culture, customs, and manners from the rest of Europe and even from Iberia's closest neighbor, France.

This was, and still is, true. Certainly, the cuisines of Spain and Portugal are unmistakably their own, and when these cuisines have traveled at all, it has been across the Atlantic to Latin America rather than across the Pyrenees.

Spain and Portugal, like most countries of southern Europe, are relatively meat-poor. Much of the land is stony and arid. It does not support large herds of beef cattle, so sheep, goats, pigs, and poultry are the main sources of meat.

The Iberians do resemble the French, however, in their very limited use of ground meat. Instead, they prefer to prepare stews utilizing bits of chicken, turkey, *chorizo* (a hard garlic-spiced Spanish sausage), rabbit, or veal, along with dried *garbanzos* (chick peas), potatoes, rice, cabbage, and other vegetables.

In fact, the *cocido,* or stew, is the national dish of Spain, while Portugal has its very similar *cozido.* Poor families simply stretch their meat supply by putting fewer chunks or smaller bits of meat into the pot, or they may leave out the meat altogether.

Fish serves as the high-protein staple of most Spanish and Portuguese people. When fresh fish is difficult to obtain, there is always dried salted codfish, which the ingenious Iberians know how to prepare in more than a hundred different ways. Soups, egg dishes, such as the Spanish *tortilla* (omelet), and vegetable dishes help to round out menus without a scrap of meat in them.

Those who can afford roasts and chops in Iberia are lucky, for all animals are slaughtered at a young and tender age because of the limited grazing land. Roast suckling pig and charcoal-grilled baby lamb are crisp, succulent specialties of Spain.

But "bullfighter's steak" is something else again, for this is the butchered meat of the special breed of Spanish fighting bull that has been killed in the ring. Although these bulls are allotted some of the best grazing land in

Spain, they are definitely not beef animals, and their meat is so tough that it must be marinated in olive oil and citrus juice before cooking.

One would expect that the meat of bulls bred for the arena (which has given beef such a bad name in Spain) would be ground up for hamburger. But again, like the French, the Spanish distrust ground meat. Perhaps this goes back to the poverty-ridden 18th and 19th centuries, when Spain lost its power, its prestige, and its empire, and when it was common practice for innkeepers to serve cat passed off as rabbit to unwary travelers. Even today rabbit is exhibited for sale in Spain's meat markets with the furry paws left on to convince customers that it is not cat!

One place you are sure to get American-style hamburgers is in the Spanish capital, Madrid, where snack bars and sidewalk cafés on the main avenues serve such un-Spanish specialties as toasted club sandwiches and *perros calientes* (hot dogs). The "hamburgers," however, are likely to be made of veal rather than the scarcer and much tougher beef.

In the more conservative Portuguese capital, Lisbon, a favorite hamburger-type lunchtime snack is the *empada,* an individual "pie" or turnover of crisp pastry filled with chopped chicken, sausage, or other meat. *Bolinhos de carne* (meat croquettes) and *merendas de carne* (large lunch rolls filled before baking with centers of ground meat) are other tasty Portuguese approaches to the hamburger idea.

ITALY   Italy says "meat balls, spaghetti, and tomato sauce" to most people. This image belittles the excellent and varied cuisine of Italy. At the same time it glamorizes the daily diet of most spaghetti-eating Italians.

Americans have received most of their impressions of Italian food from family-operated restaurants, the proprietors of which emigrated chiefly from southern Italy where *pasta* (spaghetti, macaroni, lasagne, ravioli, etc.) is a staple food and a favorite sauce ingredient is the tomato, which was brought to Europe from America by the Spanish conquerors in the 16th century.

Once established in America, Italian restauranteurs added large hearty meatballs or quantities of chopped beef to their spaghetti dishes in order to please meat-eating Americans.

However, among the numerous poor of southern Italy, many of whom live in rude country huts or in teeming city tenements, *pasta* is a staple, but meat is a rarity. The land is spiny with mountain ridges, and the steeply-sloping farmlands are cut into steplike terraces. Only sheep, goats, and donkeys can be grazed. Cattle are rare, and ground meat for sauce is almost as scarce as beef-steak. Even a meatless tomato sauce or a little grated cheese for the daily spaghetti may be beyond the family's means.

The everyday dish of many Italians is *pasta e fagiole,* a soupy stew of *pasta* and dried beans such as chick peas, broad beans, and lentils. This dish is rendered even more economical if it is made with broken odds and ends of the various shapes and sizes of *pasta,* which can usually be bought cheaply at the back door of the local spaghetti factory.

In northern Italy the poor depend largely on rice, which is grown in the Po River valley, and on *polenta,* a porridge of boiled cornmeal, made from the maize of the American Indian, which is now widely grown in Europe.

Vegetables, fish (including dried, salted cod), cheeses, an occasional bit of salami or other sausage, garlic, olive oil, and various bread products make up the daily menus for most Italians. Pizza originated as a coarse, filling bread of Naples, smeared with tomato paste and sprinkled with cheese.

The desire for a little meat in the diet has led to the tradition of eating small birds such as quails, thrushes, and blackbirds. These can commonly be purchased at street markets throughout Italy and have earned that land a reputation as the place "where songbirds are regarded as delicatessen."

Of course, those who can afford it eat exceedingly well in Italy. Because of limited grazing land, even in the dairy-rich north, veal is slaughtered while it is still being milk-fed and lends itself to delectable veal *scaloppine* dishes—breaded, herbed, sauced in wine, or served with melted cheese on top. The city of Florence boasts of its *bistecca,* tender beefsteak from young steers. Bologna stuffs its small ravioli-like *pasta,* called *tortellini,* with a mixture of very finely ground pork, veal, and chicken, and then cooks them in cream. And it makes its famous Bolognese *ragù* sauce for noodles with plenty of mixed chopped meat, finely-cut vegetables, and only a little tomato paste.

Known as the center for the richest eating in all of Italy, Bologna makes a baked *lasagne* that is very different from that of Naples and the south, layering the large broad noodles with a thick *ragù* and disdaining tomato sauce in favor of a creamy white sauce and plenty of cheese.

However, on holidays and special family occasions even the humble of Italy find the means to celebrate. Carnival time in Naples calls for a baked *lasagne* with a really meat-rich tomato sauce, and Easter in Rome means roast baby lamb or roast milk-fed kid, for, as in so many other meat-poor countries of the world, meat is the measure of luxury eating.

NEAPOLITAN LASAGNE (Italy)

10 strips uncooked lasagne noodles
1 15-ounce container ricotta cheese (or 1 pound
   small-curd creamed cottage cheese)
1 egg, beaten
½ teaspoon salt
⅛ teaspoon white pepper
1 ½ tablespoons butter or margarine
3 cups Italian meat sauce (see recipe that follows)
½ pound mozzarella cheese, cut in thin slices (or ½
   pound sweet Muenster cheese)
½ cup grated Parmesan cheese

Cook lasagne noodles as directed on package. After draining, set lasagne aside in water just to cover, to prevent sticking together. Set oven to heat to 325 degrees Fahrenheit.

In a medium-size bowl combine ricotta cheese, egg, salt, and pepper. Beat together with wire whisk.

Lightly butter a 9x13 aluminum pan or glass baking dish that has a rim 2 inches high. Place a few tablespoons of the meat sauce in the baking dish and spread it to lightly cover the bottom.

Arrange 3 strips lasagne in baking dish to form a covering layer. Spoon one-third of the ricotta mixture on top. Cover with one-third of the meat sauce. Arrange one-third of the mozzarella slices on top of the meat sauce. Sprinkle with one-third of the grated Parmesan cheese.

Repeat procedure two times, using 4 slightly overlapping strips of lasagne for the topmost layer. Dot top with the remainder of the 1 ½ tablespoons butter. Bake at 325 degrees for 45 minutes. Let baked *lasagne* stand in a warm place for 5 to 10 minutes. Cut in squares and serve.

Makes 8 to 10 servings. MENU SUGGESTION: serve NEAPOLITAN LASAGNE with a salad of torn romaine lettuce leaves in an oil-and-vinegar dressing, and with garlic bread. To prepare garlic bread, butter slices of Italian bread, sprinkle lightly with garlic salt, and toast golden-brown on a large shallow baking pan in a 375-degree oven.

ITALIAN MEAT SAUCE

- 2 tablespoons olive oil or salad oil
- 1 medium-large onion, cut in very small pieces
- 1 large clove garlic, mashed or put through garlic press
- ¾ pound hamburger
- 1 ½ teaspoons salt
- ⅛ teaspoon black pepper
- ½ teaspoon dried oregano
- ½ teaspoon dried basil
- 1 28-ounce can Italian-style plum tomatoes, with their liquid
- 1 6-ounce can tomato paste

Heat oil in a deep 10-inch skillet over medium-high heat. Add onion and garlic. Cook, stirring with wooden spoon, until pale golden-brown. Crumble hamburger into skillet. Continue cooking just until it loses its red color.

Add remaining ingredients and stir to blend. When contents of skillet are beginning to bubble, reduce heat to low. Simmer sauce, uncovered, for 35 to 45 minutes or until thickened, stirring from time to time.

Makes 4 to 4 ½ cups sauce. MENU SUGGESTION: use ITALIAN MEAT SAUCE in recipe for NEAPOLITAN LASAGNE or serve over spaghetti or other pasta cooked according to directions on package. Unused sauce may be stored in refrigerator for one week or in freezer for two to three months. Store in a covered glass or plastic container.

GREECE AND TURKEY   Greece, with its rocky, sun-baked hillsides, is similar in its climate and terrain to other Mediterranean coastal countries of Europe. Even in ancient times, the Greeks suffered from overpopulation of their small, rugged mainland and their hundreds of tiny, stony-soiled islands, lacking in adequate farmland and animal pasturage. This resulted in Greek colonization of other coastal territories, ranging as far east as Asia Minor and as far west as the Iberian peninsula.

As might be expected, beef cattle are scarce in Greece, and sheep and goats are the main sources of meat. The staple foods of the poor are dried beans, rice, some types of macaroni, vegetables, and, of course, fish from the surrounding seas.

The Greek equivalent of the *cocido* of Spain and the *pasta e fagiole* of Italy is *fava,* a stew of dried split-peas seasoned with onion, garlic, and oregano, and enriched with a dash of olive oil. This dish, always made with some type of dried legume, is as old as the Acropolis, for it has a long history as the everyday fare of the Grecian poor.

When meat is available, it is used sparingly, as in a Greek lamb stew or a baked lamb dish, the bulk of which is made up of vegetables ranging from artichokes to zucchini. City-dwelling Greeks are great lovers of street snacks. In Athens, the equivalent of the American hamburger-on-a-bun is *souvlakia me pitta,* chunks or slices of spit-roasted lamb sandwiched into a folded over circle of "Arab" or Middle Eastern style pancake bread, along with pieces of tomato, onion, and shredded salad greens.

Souvlakia is the Greek version of the Turkish *shish-kebab,* meaning "sword meat," as the Turkish horsemen of the plains are reputed to have impaled chunks of raw meat on their swords for roasting over open fires.

In Istanbul, Athens, and most recently in New York, the type of *souvlakia* that is skillfully cut from a large revolving cone of lamb impaled on an upright spit has become very popular. The turning meat is exposed to a vertical charcoal fire placed at the back of the spit. As the tastily-browned, dripping meat is shaved away, the newly-exposed portion begins to brown. The cone of lamb gradually diminishes in size, as it is carved closer and closer to the spit.

The Greeks and the Turks have a long history of animosity, for the Turks were masters of Greece for nearly 400 years, beginning in 1460. At the same time, they have a shared culture, so that many of their dishes and the general flavor of their cuisines are very similar, if not interchangeable. Greek *dolmades* (vine leaves, peppers, tomatoes, or other vegetables, stuffed with rice or with a mixture of rice and ground lamb) are almost ex-

actly the same as the many kinds of Turkish *dolmas.*
Both countries prepare *moussaka,* a baked dish of ground
lamb layered with slices of eggplant, potato, or zucchini
squash. And both make flaky cheese-filled turnovers and
savory cheese pies out of layers of paper-thin pastry
called *phyllo.*

The Turks are a Moslem people to whom pork is forbidden. Oddly enough, although the Greek Orthodox religion does not prohibit pork, the Greeks seem to have
retained the Turkish influence, for they produce and eat
very little pork. Lamb remains the Greek festival dish,
particularly at Easter when the Lenten fast is broken at
midnight with an egg-and-lemon flavored soup made with
lamb parts, to be followed by an Easter Sunday dinner of
spit-roasted whole baby lamb.

MOUSSAKA (*Greece and Turkey*)

4 *medium-large potatoes (about 2 pounds)*
2 *tablespoons olive oil or salad oil*
1 *large onion, cut in very small pieces*
1 *clove garlic, mashed or put through garlic press*
1 *pound lean ground lamb, or hamburger*
1 *cup, canned or bottled, thick tomato sauce (type
   used for spaghetti)*
½ *teaspoon dried oregano*
1 *teaspoon dried parsley*
1 *teaspoon salt*
  pinch black pepper
4 *tablespoons fine dried bread crumbs*
3 *tablespoons butter*

1 ½ cups milk
* 4 tablespoons flour*
* ½ teaspoon salt*
* 1 egg*
* 6 tablespoons grated Parmesan cheese*

Pare potatoes and cut into slices ¼ inch thick. In a
large covered saucepan (6-cup size), bring 3 cups of
water and 2 teaspoons salt to a boil. Add potato slices
and cook 15 minutes or until just tender. Carefully pour
off water and put saucepan back on warm cooking unit
(with heat turned off) to dry potatoes thoroughly. Put
potatoes into bowl, without breaking slices, and set aside.
Wash out saucepan for re-use.

In a deep 10-inch skillet, heat oil over medium heat.
Add onion and garlic and cook, stirring with wooden
spoon, until pale golden-brown. Crumble meat into skillet and continue cooking until it loses its red color. Add
tomato sauce, oregano, parsley, the 1 teaspoon salt, pepper, and bread crumbs. Remove from heat and set aside.

Set oven to heat to 350 degrees Fahrenheit. Melt the
butter in the large saucepan in which the potatoes were
cooked. Add ¾ cup of the milk. To the remaining ¾
cup milk, add flour and stir until perfectly smooth. Add
this mixture to saucepan. Add the ½ teaspoon salt. Cook
over medium-high heat, stirring frequently with a wooden
spoon until mixture is thick and smooth. If lumps appear, beat with wire whisk. In a medium-size mixing
bowl, beat the egg. Add thickened milk mixture to bowl,
a little at a time, beating constantly with wire whisk.

Lightly butter a 9x13 aluminum pan or glass baking
dish that has a rim 2 inches high. Arrange half of the

potato slices on the bottom of the pan. Spoon on half the meat mixture. Repeat. Spoon the thickened milk sauce over all, covering the meat. Then sprinkle the grated cheese on top. Bake at 350 degrees for 30 to 35 minutes, or until top is puffy and golden-brown. To serve, cut in squares.

Makes 6 servings. MENU SUGGESTION: serve MOUS-SAKA with a Greek-style salad of chunks of tomato, green pepper, cucumber, black olives, and other vegetables in a tangy oil-and-lemon dressing.

YUGOSLAVIA, ROMANIA, AND BULGARIA

Greece and European Turkey share the Balkan peninsula of southeastern Europe with Yugoslavia, Romania, Bulgaria, and Albania. These Balkan nations have communist forms of government. Although differing somewhat in philosophy and practice, each is dedicated to the elimination of hunger in a traditionally poor and strife-torn Balkan land.

Yugoslavia, "land of the south Slavs," eats particularly well now compared to the years before World War II when it was a monarchy. The country has not one but *four* principal cuisines, based on regional and historical influences.

Along the Adriatic coast in the region known as Dalmatia, fish is the mainstay. In the interior mountains of Bosnia and Herzegovina, where the Turks held sway for nearly 450 years and where there are still many Moslem

converts, lamb is the principal meat. It is eaten somewhat sparingly, however, and is made to go a long way
with the help of vegetables, rice, and bread grains.

In the green and fertile Alpine foothills of the Yugoslav region of Slovenia, close to the Austrian border,
considerable veal and pork is produced for delicate
schnitzels, tender fillet slices of meat that are usually
breaded and fried. Farther east, in Serbia, the historical
heartland of Yugoslavia, grilled meats are the great spe-
cialty.

The Yugoslav version of the hamburger is a small
"sausage" of freshly ground beef (or beef mixed with
veal and/or pork), about the size of a cocktail frank-
furter. These are called *ćevapčići* (tschev-ap'-chee-tchee)
and are often grilled over charcoal at outdoor garden
restaurants. Served half a dozen at a clip, they are always

eaten with chopped raw onion and stinging little hot peppers.

Even more hamburger-like is *pljeskavica* (plyes'-ka-vee-tsa), the same type of ground meat shaped into a very large flat patty and grilled. *Pljeskavica* may be eaten with thick chunks of firm-crusted Serbian bread, and always with raw onion and fiery peppers, but it is never sandwiched into a bun or roll.

Romania, Yugoslavia's neighbor, has its *mititei* which are almost exactly like *ćevapčići* except that they are highly seasoned with garlic, which is a favorite in this Latin-influenced Balkan country, many of whose inhabitants trace their origins back to the ancient Romans. Romania's grassy Danube plains and lush Transylvanian valleys afford good grazing for cattle and other meat animals, and excellent beefsteaks are available.

Of course, like most southern Europeans, the majority of Romanians have to find diet mainstays that are less expensive than meat. Like the Italians, they are particularly fond of cornmeal dishes, and they eat this American Indian food as a porridge, with eggs, cheese, or fish, with meat stews, and even boiled, sliced, and fried. The Romanian *polenta* is called *mamaliga*.

Bulgarians eat a diet closer to that of Greece and Turkey. Sheep are the main source of meat, supplemented with many whole grains, vegetables, and a great deal of yogurt, which was once thought to be the reason why Bulgarians are so long-lived! Like all Balkan peoples, the Bulgarians use ground meats, usually lamb, very cleverly in combination with rice and vegetables in all sorts of *dolmas* and *moussakas*, thus creating some of the tastiest meat-stretching dishes in the world.

HAMBURGER COOKERY IN AFRICA

NORTH AFRICA   The Sahara Desert sweeps across the northern third of the African continent, separating the Mediterranean coast from the rest of Africa by more than mere distance.

The North African coastal countries are closely related in their culture to the Arab Middle East. Most of the inhabitants of Egypt, Libya, Tunisia, Algeria, and Morocco speak Arabic and follow the Moslem religion. Only the coastal fringes of these countries are naturally fertile. Just beyond the cultivated fields and the congested cities, each clustered around its ancient citadel or *casbah,* lie the sands of the Sahara. The desert's arid dunelands, bare plateaus, and stony outcroppings are broken only by an occasional oasis fed by a mysterious underground stream.

With careful irrigation and cultivation, some oases can support a good-sized village, with grain and vegetable patches, date palms, and grazing areas for sheep and camels. The true desert nomad, however, wanders between the desert oases and the coastal settlements, trading the hair and hides of his camels for dates, wheat, and other agricultural products. He hunts the desert gazelle for meat, drinks camel's milk, and also eats the dry, coarse meat of the camel.

In the coastal towns and villages, North Africans live on grains and vegetables, with lamb the principal meat, as in most Moslem countries. The favorite cereal grain is *couscous* (koos'-koos), tiny pellets of coarsely milled wheat or millet. *Couscous* is cooked with water until the grains are tender and then steamed so that it is moist and sticky enough to be eaten with the fingers, simply by rolling it into a ball and popping it into the mouth.

North Africans usually eat their *couscous* with a lamb or chicken stew that has plenty of vegetables in it, and often chick peas, walnuts, raisins, and pomegranate seeds as well. The diner sits on the floor at a low table. After forming the ball of *couscous* he rolls it around in the stew picking up tidbits of vegetables and meat. All of this must be accomplished with the right hand, for throughout most of Africa and Asia the left hand is considered reserved for bodily functions and must not be used at table.

The "hamburger" of the North African (and throughout Middle Eastern countries of Asia such as Syria, Lebanon, Jordan, Iraq, and Iran) is *kefta,* usually ground lamb, sometimes ground beef, seasoned to the regional taste with a wide assortment of spices. *Kefta* are shaped as meat balls, patties, or "fingers," and are grilled or fried. *Kefta* and *kebabs* (chunks of grilled lamb) are not the daily fare of most North Africans but are reserved for important occasions.

An interesting luxury dish of Algeria and Morocco is *pastilla,* usually translated as "pigeon pie." *Pastilla* is made up of tens of layers of thin, flaky *phyllo* pastry crammed with chopped or finely cut cooked pigeon, chicken, or lamb, along with eggs, nuts, and spices, including cinnamon. Oddly enough, the pie is sprinkled with finely powdered sugar before serving. A sumptuous North African meal might open with *pastilla,* followed by *couscous* with a meaty lamb stew and then by roast lamb or mutton.

Some of the richest eating in North Africa is done during the religious fasting month of Ramadan, the most important of the Moslem holidays. During this ninth month of the Moslem calendar year, no food or water may be taken between the hours of sun-up and sundown.

However, once the sunset gun has boomed its message

of release from fasting for the day, rich and poor alike fall to their nightly eating. Vendors appear on the streets toward sunset, selling *herrira* soup with which many people break the day's fast. This thick, hearty soup is made with chick peas, vegetables, and spices, and usually contains bits of chicken and lamb.

A *kefta* preparation of meatroll slices and hard-cooked eggs, breaded and fried like croquettes, is a popular main dish at the nightly fast-breaking meal during Ramadan. As North Africans are very fond of mint, mint tea, sweetened with a great deal of sugar, is a principal beverage at meals and in between. Mint is also added to the North African fresh vegetable salads of tomatoes, peppers, and cucumbers that usually accompany *keftas* and stews, and it is even added to the chopped meat for *kefta* itself.

MEATROLL-AND-EGG CROQUETTES (*North Africa*)

1 ½ pounds ground lean lamb, or hamburger
1 large clove garlic, mashed or put through garlic press
1 ½ teaspoons salt
¼ teaspoon white pepper
1 teaspoon finely-cut fresh mint, or 2 teaspoons dried crumbled mint leaves
3 hard-cooked eggs, shelled
  flour
1 egg, beaten with 1 tablespoon cold water
  fine, dried bread crumbs
  salad oil

Combine ground lamb or hamburger, garlic, salt, pepper, and mint. Place meat mixture on a sheet of wax paper. Cover with another sheet of wax paper and pat or roll out the meat into a 9-inch square, about ½ inch thick.

Remove top sheet of wax paper. Lay the three hard-cooked eggs, end to end, on the edge of the square nearest you. Roll up the meat over the eggs and away from you, using the bottom sheet of wax paper to help shape the meat into a long, thick roll. Slice the meat roll, cutting through the eggs in the center, to make 8 round slices, each a little over one inch thick. Lay the meat-and-egg rounds down flat and pat meat snugly around the egg slice in center to hold it in place.

Coat each round with flour, then dip it into the beaten egg mixture, and then coat thoroughly with bread crumbs.

In a deep 10-inch skillet, heat enough salad oil to cover the bottom to a depth of ¼ inch. Add the meatroll-and-egg slices to the hot oil and fry on one side until brown and crusty. Turn and fry on other side. Drain on paper toweling and serve at once.

Makes 4 to 6 servings. MENU SUGGESTION: serve MEATROLL-AND-EGG CROQUETTES with a spicy tomato sauce or with ketchup or chili sauce. As accompaniments serve rice and a salad of chunks of tomato, green pepper, and cucumber dressed with oil, lemon juice, and snips of fresh mint or crumbled dried mint.

AFRICA SOUTH OF THE SAHARA   The vast bulk of Africa lying south of the Sahara has a terrain ranging from equatorial jungle to lofty grassland and snow-capped mountains. Some of the world's largest game animals roam the high plains of East Africa, while herding peoples such as the Masai of Kenya and Tanzania own numerous head of cattle. Yet the inhabitants of East, West, Central, and South Africa are among the most meat-poor and protein-hungry of the world's peoples.

This is explained in part by the rapidly growing population and increased restrictions against the killing of many dwindling animal species.

In addition, most of Africa's herding peoples refuse to slaughter their cattle except on rare occasions. Cattle-ownership is a mark of wealth and prestige. Cattle buy brides for a man's sons and extra wives for himself, should he desire them. As quantity is the all-important factor, breeding for improved quality or trimming the herd in times of drought and poor grazing is not considered.

Besides, the animals provide milk and blood, the mainstays of certain tribal diets. The Masai and others regularly draw blood from the neck veins of their cattle, which they drink combined with milk.

Poaching is practiced rather widely, of course, by the meat-hungry Africans. And any wild animal that wanders outside the limits of the government game reserve

or plays havoc with an African's domesticated herds is considered fair game for the cooking pot. This means that hippopotamus and elephant, buffalo and antelope, as well as ostrich and crocodile, dogs and monkeys, rats and mice, and even locusts and termites (fried crisp in oil) are eaten at one time or another by people in Africa.

The meat from a large kill is devoured quickly among Africans, for there are few ways of preserving it out in the bush except by drying. To accomplish this, the meat must be cut in thin, narrow strips or "tongues" and dried in the sun. The hard leathery dried meat is known as biltong and is very similar to the jerky of the American Indians. Africa's biltong, however, is likely to be prepared from the coarse flesh of elephant or from the meat of zebra, eland, or gazelle.

The meat of most game animals and even of domesticated ones in Africa is tough, even when cut quite small and cooked in stews as is often done. But many tribal peoples believe that a man takes on the qualities of the animal he eats and so, given a choice, prefer the meat of the larger, braver, and fiercer species of game. Chicken, for this reason, is not particularly favored even though poultry is easy to raise and an excellent source of protein.

For the most part, Africans subsist on grains such as millet, corn, and sorghum, and on porridges and mushes prepared from these and from the cassava root, the cooking banana, and the local varieties of yam and sweet potato. Unfortunately, all of these are low in protein and are quite flavorless and dull as well.

The African yam is a large, starchy root vegetable, much less nutritious than the moist golden sweet potato familiar to most Americans. The cassava, the starchy root of the manioc plant, is a very popular staple because it is easy to grow and so long-keeping that it can tide Africans over a famine period, such as might result from a grain-crop failure.

In West Africa, a thick mash called *garri* is made from dried, pounded cassava, and a porridge called *fufu* is made from ground millet. Plantain, a large banana-like fruit that must be cooked to be eaten, is boiled or cut in slices and fried in palm oil, which turns it red.

Moyinmoyin is a West African dish of mashed dried beans or black-eyed peas, seasoned with hot red peppers. Sometimes dried fish (a helpful source of protein for West Africans) is added, or meat if it is available. Peanuts (which Africans call groundnuts, as do the British), roasted and ground, make a stew with vegetables, water, spices, and occasionally some meat. Stews are always stretched with plenty of *garri,* mashed yams, or boiled plantain in West Africa. The peppery flavor of the stew helps to perk up the stodgy taste of the rib-sticking, but not very nutritious, starchy food.

Ugali, a cornmeal or millet porridge, is the *fufu* of the East Africans, whose diet is fairly similar to that of West Africans—cassava, groundnuts, dried beans, tomatoes, squash, and the occasional stew with a bit of meat in it.

East Africa grows a short, plump, green cooking banana that is smaller than the West African plantain. Green bananas (or bananas of the sweet yellow variety, cooked while they are still green and hard) are cut into chunks and used in meat and vegetable stews in the same way that turnips, carrots, and potatoes are used in North American stews. East Africans consider the sweet ripe banana a snack food for children. Adults seldom eat them except when on safari, since they make suitable picnic food.

Green bananas are high in starch content and not sweet. A staple dish among East Africans and Central Africans is *matoke*. It is made by boiling the peeled green banana in water until soft and then mashing it. *Matoke* is so low in protein that young children who are weaned from mother's milk and put on a diet of *matoke* develop a serious protein-deficiency disease called kwashiorkor.

In East Africa the food is less "hot" than in West Africa, with the exception of Ethiopia where *berberi*, powdered red pepper, adds a fiery note to most dishes and is considered an antidote to the parasites in the raw meat that Ethiopians traditionally eat.

However, with 25 million head of cattle—one to every person in Ethiopia—meat is still not plentiful, because of the seemingly universal African preference for keeping beef on the hoof.

Ethiopia has a unique cuisine consisting mainly of *injera,* a flexible spongy pancake bread made from millet flour, and *wat,* a peppery stew of onions and other vegetables, with beef, lamb, or chicken added to it on occasion. The Ethiopian eats his food from a large round tray set atop a table of woven basketry. Pieces of the overlapping layers of *injera,* ladled with *wat,* are torn off to serve as edible scoops for conveying the stew meat, vegetables, and gravy to the mouth. No knife, fork, spoon, plate, or even napkin is ever required, with all-purpose *injera* on hand.

Although the Ethiopians are predominantly Christians, they resemble most other Africans in that they do not raise pigs. Many Africans south of the Sahara are Moslems by conversion, and there is also a large Asian Moslem population living in East Africa, all of whom are prohibited from eating pork.

Among the native peoples of southern Africa, a grain sorghum called kaffir-corn or mealie makes a ground cereal for the daily porridge. Probably the only real "hamburger" recipe of southern Africa came from its white, ruling-class Dutch settlers, known as Afrikaners. This Malay-influenced dish from Indonesia, where the Dutch were long-time rulers, is really a sort of sweet-and-sour baked meat loaf called *bobotie*. It is made with ground lamb or beef, eggs, onions, bread, curry powder, lemon juice, sugar, raisins, and almonds, and is served with rice and chutney.

But a more truly African dish would be a stew of meat and green cooking bananas from Tanzania, which in the absence of tiny cubes of goat meat or gazelle can quite satisfactorily be made with hamburger.

CHOPPED STEAK AND BANANAS (Tanzania, East Africa)

3 *tablespoons salad oil*
1 *large onion, cut in very small pieces*
1 *medium-large green pepper, cut in ½-inch squares*
3 *firm, green, unripe bananas, cut in ¾-inch-thick slices*
1 *pound hamburger*
1 *cup canned stewed tomatoes, drained of their liquid*
1 *teaspoon salt*
⅛ *teaspoon coarsely ground black pepper*

Heat oil in a deep 10-inch skillet over medium-high heat. Add onion and green pepper. Cook, stirring with a wooden spoon, until lightly browned. Add banana slices and toss lightly.

Keeping heat at medium-high, crumble hamburger over contents of skillet. Stir until it loses its red color. Reduce heat under skillet to low.

Add tomatoes, salt, and pepper. Cover skillet and simmer for about 20 minutes, or until bananas are evenly tender. (They will not become *very* soft, and they will remain slightly chewy.) Check seasoning and serve.

Makes 5 to 6 servings. MENU SUGGESTION: serve CHOPPED STEAK AND BANANAS over peanut rice, prepared as follows. Cook ¾ cup raw rice according to directions on package. When tender, add ¼ cup shelled, roasted peanuts, which have been chopped fine, and 1 tablespoon butter. Season to taste with onion salt or seasoned salt.

AMBURGER
COOKERY IN ASIA

THE MIDDLE EAST   Asia, the world's largest continent, is the home of over half the world's people. Its land
mass contains the two most populous nations on earth:
India with about 600 million and China with about 800
million. Rice and wheat are the principal crops and the
almost exclusive staff of life for tens of millions of Asians.
Meat of any kind is a rarity for most. But many regions
do have distinctive cuisines in which hamburger or other
ground meat plays its usual useful role. The Middle East
is one such place.

The term "Middle East" generally means southwest
Asia, from Asiatic Turkey as far south as the lower tip
of the Arabian peninsula, and from the eastern end of
the Mediterranean Sea to the western borders of Pakistan
and India. Most of the land of the Middle East is parched
and arid. Even the fertile valley lands of the Tigris and
Euphrates Rivers, which saw the birth of agriculture in
about 6000 B.C., are today partly devastated by the
overgrazing of goats and sheep and by overplanting.

As in the Moslem lands of North Africa, sheep are

the principal livestock of the Middle East. Goats are raised for milk and cheese and for their wool. But their meat is seldom eaten because of the animals' customary diet of town and village refuse, which renders them unclean to the Moslem way of thinking. Unlike pork, however, goat meat is not actually forbidden to Moslems. Beef cattle are very scarce due to the lack of adequate grazing land.

Most sheep of the Middle East are of the fat-tailed variety. Fat, stored in their tails, sees them through periods of poor feeding due to drought or soil infertility, acting as a source of nourishment in time of need. In Syria and Lebanon, a well-fed, and sometimes force-fed, fat-tailed sheep grows such a heavy tail of fat that a wooden plank on wheels or runners must be fastened beneath its tail to support it as the animal ambles about. At slaughtering time, the tail fat is rendered and stored in crocks for use as cooking fat all year round. Sheep fat is really the lard and butter of the Middle East.

Wheat is the principal grain of the Middle East and is very often eaten in the form of *burghul* (also called cracked wheat and, sometimes, *bulgar*). Crunchy and nutty flavored, coarse-size *burghul* grains are a little smaller than rice kernels. They make a hearty porridge, go into a Syrian-Lebanese salad of chopped mint, parsley, onions, and tomatoes, called *tabbouleh,* and combine with the meat of fat-tailed sheep to make the "hamburger" dish of the Middle East, known as *kibbeh.*

To prepare this dish, ground lamb or mutton and ground *burghul* grains are pounded together to a paste. The mixture may be baked as a meatloaf in a shallow pan, with a middle layer of additional chopped lamb

mixed with browned onions, pine nuts, and cinnamon.
Kibbeh can also be shaped into balls or thick oblong
patties, filled with a stuffing mixture of pine nuts and
onions, and fried in oil.

Grilled *kebabs* of lamb are popular in the Middle East
as they are in North Africa. But here, too, *kefta kebabs*,
meatballs or "fingers" of ground lamb broiled on a spit,
are a practical substitution for the more costly chunks of
tender lamb.

Israel, the world's first Jewish state, created in 1948,
sits in the midst of the Arab-Moslem world. About ten
per cent of Israel's population is made up of Arab peoples.

In reclaiming the desert-like wastes of their new homeland for agriculture, the progressive Israelis have developed a new cuisine referred to as *sabra*. This is also
the name applied to all native-born Israeli men and
women.

Sabra food is less fatty than that of the neighboring
Arab lands, and less starchy than that of central and
eastern Europe where many of the first Israeli immigrants
were born. The "blooming deserts" of Israel have given
its people a diet high in fresh vegetables and fruits. Cattle
are preferred to sheep but are raised mainly as a source
of dairy products—milk, cheese, and yogurt. Poultry is

raised for eggs and also for its frequent appearance on the dinner table. Fish is another good source of protein in Israeli meals. Jews, like Moslems, do not eat pork.

Of course, nourishing Middle Eastern foods like *burghul,* eggplant, olives, honey, nuts, and chick peas are very much a part of *sabra* everyday eating. And who has not heard of *felafel,* tasty little deep-fried balls of mashed chick peas, *burghul,* and spices? Stuffed into a puffed round of Arab pancake bread, along with shredded salad greens and a dash of hot sauce, *felafel* are the non-meat street snacks of Israel, equivalent to the franks and burgers of the United States.

The beef that comes to the Israeli dinner table about once a week, as a stew, pot roast, or hamburger meat, needs to be stretched as far as possible. In *sabra* cuisine, this is often accomplished with fruit, both fresh and dried, from Israeli orchards and also with nuts, as in the case of apple-burger meat balls.

APPLE-BURGER MEAT BALLS (Israel)

½   *pound hamburger*
2   *medium-small apples (Mackintosh are best)*
1   *teaspoon onion salt*
    pinch white pepper
¼   *teaspoon ground cloves*
1   *small egg*
⅓   *cup fine dried bread crumbs*
    flour
1   *tablespoon butter or margarine*
2   *tablespoons sliced or slivered almonds*

  1 cup very hot water
  2 chicken bouillon cubes
  2 tablespoons raisins
  ¼ teaspoon lemon juice
1 ½ teaspoons cornstarch (or 1 tablespoon flour)
  1 tablespoon cold water

Cut apples into quarters, pare and core, shred on coarse side of grater, or chop or cut into very small pieces. Should yield 1 cup. In a medium-large mixing bowl, combine first 7 ingredients.

Shape hamburger mixture into balls 1 ¼ inches in diameter (about 24). Roll balls in flour to coat lightly.

Melt butter or margarine in a deep 9- or 10-inch skillet over medium heat. Add almonds, and stir with wooden spoon just until pale golden-brown. Remove with a slotted spoon and set aside. Add meat balls to skillet and brown them well on all sides. Take skillet off heat and let it cool for 5 minutes.

Add the very hot water, bouillon cubes, raisins, lemon juice, and almonds to the meat balls in skillet. Cover and simmer over medium-low heat 10 to 15 minutes.

Mix cornstarch and cold water together so that there are no lumps. Add to meat ball mixture in skillet, stirring with wooden spoon. Cook a minute or two longer, until sauce has thickened. (This dish can be made ahead of time and reheated.)

Makes 3 to 4 servings. MENU SUGGESTION: serve APPLE-BURGER MEAT BALLS with brown rice or burghul and with braised zucchini squash.

INDIA   The vast subcontinent of southern Asia, known as India, is believed to have grown the world's first rice and sugar cane and to have been the original home of what is now the barnyard chicken.

Spices were being grown in India thousands of years ago, making it the center of world demand for these important food preservatives. So it is not surprising that to most people today Indian food means curry.

Curry is not one spice but many, and its flavor varies according to the kinds and proportions of spices and herbs that are freshly ground or pounded together on a particular day by the Indian housewife. Some of the most common curry ingredients are cumin, coriander, turmeric (which gives curry its yellow color), and fenugreek (which gives it its characteristic odor), along with pepper, cloves, cardamom, ginger, mace, fennel, mustard, and so forth.

The spice that gives some curries their stinging hot taste (for there are mild curries and strong curries) comes, oddly enough, from the sharp-flavored capsicum or pod peppers, sometimes called chilies, that were found growing in America by the discoverers of the New World and were brought to India by the Portuguese. Commercially prepared, pre-packaged curry powder is mainly used outside India. For non-Indian cooks it usually offers a reasonable substitute, although the flavors of the spices will not, of course, be as fresh as in the home-ground variety.

For Indians, most of whom live on a diet of rice, lentils, vegetables, and *chappatis* (thin pancake-like bread rounds), curry adds flavor and a little change to an otherwise very dull daily menu. Many Indians are vegetarians by necessity; others by choice. Hindus (about 83 per cent of the population) will not eat beef, as cattle are considered sacred in their religion; Moslems (about 10 per cent of the population) will not eat pork; and some sects will not eat vegetables grown beneath the ground, because they do not wish to deprive worms and similar creatures of *their* dinner. Among Hindus, there are vegetarians so strict that they refuse all foods that have ever contained the germ of animal life, such as eggs.

Mohandas K. Gandhi, the great Indian independence leader, was a Hindu who observed strict vegetarianism until the age of thirteen when he was persuaded by a Moslem friend to try goat meat. Although he soon returned to a life of vegetarianism, Gandhi (who never grew beyond five feet, five inches) apparently believed that it was meat eating that gave the British rulers of India their physical superiority. He often quoted a popular Indian jingle:

> *Behold the mighty Englishman—*
> *He rules the Indian small,*
> *Because being a meat-eater*
> *He is five cubits tall.*

A cubit is about eighteen inches. This would make the Englishman seven-and-a-half feet tall, which is, of course, an exaggeration.

Indian food varies somewhat according to region. In the north, wheat is the staple. Rice is also eaten but not as much as in the south where it is the mainstay. *Chappatis*, as well as fried breads called *parathas* and *pooris*, are made from wheat flour in northern India. *Poppadums*, on the other hand, are crisp, waferlike breads made from rice flour and lentil flour and are eaten throughout India. *Ghee,* or clarified butter, is used in cooking mainly in the north, while the south uses oils extracted from coconut and sesame seed, and the east uses mustard-seed oil. Coastal people naturally eat more fish than inlanders.

In the very hot climate of southern India, the curried dishes tend to be hotter. This is explained, in part, by the fact that meats, fish, and other perishable foods spoil even more quickly here and require heavier spicing for preservation. It is also possible that highly seasoned foods serve as an appetite stimulant in a hot climate, although it is not likely that the ever-hungry masses of India need much encouragement for eating, beyond the food itself.

Lamb and chicken are the most popular meats for curries, although there are beef curries, eaten by the more emancipated. A curry with chunks or *kebabs* of meat in it is called a *korma* curry, while a curry with meatballs in it is called a *kofta* curry. *Kofta* is simply the Indian way of referring to the *kefta* of the Middle East and North Africa. A curry with loose ground meat in it is a *keema* curry. And, naturally, there are duck curries, hard-cooked egg curries, fish curries, shrimp curries, and vegetable curries.

A curry dish is really a well-seasoned stew. It is eaten with rice and almost always with *dhal:* lentils, split peas, or other dried legumes cooked with water and mild flavorings to a purée or a loose mash. *Dhal* adds valuable protein to the vegetarian diets of many Indians. *Chappatis,* yogurt, and a relish, such as pickles or chutney, complete the accompaniments to Indian curry. Chutneys —tangy, hot, or mild—are often made from India's wide selection of fruits, such as mangoes, coconuts, lemons or limes, or from green tomatoes or other vegetables.

Traditionally, Indians squat on the floor to eat their meals, which may be served on a tray on the floor or from a low table. A banana leaf may serve as a plate, and the food is eaten with the fingers of the right hand. *Chappati* or other bread serves as a scoop.

A food in which ground meat turns up, other than *kofta* or *keema* curry is the *samosa,* a deep-fried pastry turnover made with a dough of flour, *ghee,* and yogurt, and filled with ground lamb or possibly ground beef. The meat inside the turnover is, of course, well seasoned with curry ingredients. *Samosas* make popular street snacks in India and are also very well-liked as a savory at British-style afternoon teas.

KEEMA CURRY (India)

 4 *tablespoons butter*
 2 *medium onions, cut in small pieces*
 1 *large clove garlic, mashed or put through garlic press*
1 ½ *tablespoons curry powder*
 1 *pound ground lamb, or hamburger*
 ½ *teaspoon ground ginger*
 ¼ *teaspoon ground cloves*
1 ½ *cups diced, peeled canned or fresh tomatoes*
 ⅓ *cup canned tomato liquid or tomato juice*
 ¾ *cup frozen green peas*
1 ½ *teaspoons salt*
 1 *crumbled bay leaf*

Heat butter in a deep 10-inch skillet. Add onions, garlic, and curry powder. Cover skillet and cook over low heat for 10 to 15 minutes until onion is very tender.

Bring heat under skillet to medium-high. Crumble ground lamb or hamburger over onion-curry mixture. Sprinkle with ginger and cloves, and stir with wooden spoon until meat loses its red color.

Add tomatoes, tomato liquid, peas, salt, and bay leaf. Cover skillet and simmer over medium-low heat for 15 to 20 minutes, or until peas are tender.

Makes 5 to 6 servings. MENU SUGGESTION: serve KEEMA CURRY with rice. A good cold side dish would be eggplant, cut in ½-inch cubes and fried tender in vegetable oil, seasoned with garlic salt and a little cayenne pepper, and mixed with chilled yogurt. Use about 1 pound of eggplant and ½ to 1 cup yogurt.

CHINA AND JAPAN What do the people of China eat? Lin Yutang, the Chinese writer and scholar, once wrote of pre-Revolutionary China: "The answer is that we eat all edible things on earth. We eat crabs by preference, and often eat barks by necessity."

There is certainly a wide range of dishes in the Chinese cuisine, some of which may go back as far as the first dynasty, the Shang, which probably arose in about 1500 B.C. They include such exotic items as "hundred-year-old" eggs (aged, blackened eggs that have probably been buried for several months at most) and bird's-nest soup (containing not nests but a gelatinous substance secreted by certain oriental swifts to hold their nests together).

On the other hand, Chinese food has such broad appeal that there is hardly a city anywhere in the world without at least a few Chinese restaurants.

Grains and vegetables are of course basic to the Chinese diet. In the southern half of this vast country, rice is the staple. Eaten mainly as boiled or steamed rice grains, it also yields rice flour, rice wine, and other products. In the northern half of the country, wheat, millet, and sorghum are the main grains, eaten largely as noodle products of both the crisp and the soft variety. Noodles are really the "steamed bread" of China.

Soybeans form a third staple. They are native to the Orient and have probably been grown there, along with rice and other cereal grasses, for as long as 5000 years. For the many Chinese who have little or no meat in their diet, the soybean is a good source of high-quality protein and also contains calcium. This amazing little legume provides bean curd, meal, flour, bean paste, bean sprouts, oil, and soy sauce, of which it is an ingredient. It even makes a tangy, strong-smelling "cheese" known as *foo yu,* which is derived from fermented bean curd.

As the Chinese do not as a rule eat dairy products, *foo yu* is a very rare cheese indeed. The traditional Chinese rejection of milk, butter, and cheese has never been satisfactorily explained. Some say it is because their long-time enemies, the Mongols, were a herding people whose mainstay was soured milk (the Tartars, "inventors" of the hamburger, were Mongols).

Of course, some Chinese who keep herds do eat dairy products. Also, Western influence is growing in China as worldwide business and cultural exchanges increase. The Japanese, to whom dairy products were also little known at one time, have become milk-drinkers and ice cream-lovers since their contacts with Americans.

China's principal meat is pork, and ground pork is undoubtedly the "hamburger" of China, for those who can afford it. It is used in soups, in dumplings such as *wonton,* in egg rolls, and simply as meat balls and crumbled ground meat in main dishes. Next to pork, chicken and duck are popular. Beef is less common, as oxen are used for farm work and are considered too valuable to be slaughtered for food. Of course, fish and shellfish are very well-liked in China wherever they are available.

The Chinese are believed to have domesticated the wild pig thousands of years ago, and it is no accident that Charles Lamb laid the setting for his essay *A Dissertation upon Roast Pig* in China. According to this tale, roast pig was discovered by chance when the foolish son of a swineherd set the family hut on fire, cooking nine young piglets to a delicious crispness. Soon, people

all over the region began burning down their houses, always making certain there was a litter of young pigs under the roof at the time.

In actuality, the Chinese show extreme wisdom in their approach to cookery. Lacking an abundance of fuel, they developed the art of cutting meats and vegetables into small strips, squares, or slices, uniform in size and shape for a specific dish, and of cooking vegetables only to a point where they were still crisp and fresh-tasting. They also learned to cook with only as much liquid as could later be incorporated into the finished dish, as a tasty sauce, thus preserving vitamins and minerals.

There are a number of different regional cuisines in China. The one best known to Americans is that of the province of Canton in southern China, although the fiery dishes of Szechuan and the less hot Hunan cookery are becoming better known outside China.

Canton Province is the home of "stir-fry" cookery, which is traditionally done in a *wok,* a large bowl-shaped pan designed to sit into the fire-hole of a Chinese stove. In stir-frying, a small amount of properly cut food is tossed into a very little hot oil at the bottom of the *wok.* It is stirred and soon pushed to the sides to cook in steam and in its own juices, while additional raw ingredients are added to the hot oil in the center of the *wok.*

Confucius is said to have recommended a proportion of one-fourth meat and three-fourths vegetables in such dishes. The variety in textures and flavors of Chinese vegetables, ranging from celery cabbage to water chestnuts and from bean sprouts to snow peas, makes it an interesting and rewarding challenge for the Chinese to stretch their limited meat supply.

The Japanese, with food traditions somewhat similar to those of the Chinese, have had to accommodate to living on a group of tiny islands instead of on a large land mass. Not surprisingly, they have turned to the sea to supplement their diet of rice, tea, vegetables, and pickles, adding varieties of fish and seaweed.

In Japan, too, ingredients are often cut small and cooked for the shortest time possible to conserve fuel. Many foods are eaten raw. Occidental peoples are often astonished at the Japanese liking for *sashimi* (thinly sliced raw fish), forgetting that clams and oysters eaten raw are widely accepted in most Western countries.

The Japanese eat about 70 pounds of fish per person per year, but only 10 pounds of meat (while the United States eats only 10 pounds of fish per person per year).

With the opening of Japan to the West in the mid-19th century, cattle were imported, mainly so that foreign residents could have beef at their tables. *Sukiyaki*, a dish of beef and vegetables cut in thin strips, is cooked and served in Japanese fashion, but is not truly a traditional dish of Japan.

The growing prosperity of the Japanese people today has spurred a desire for more meat, particularly beef. Lacking grazing land, the Japanese some years ago developed a special type of beef cattle, usually identified as Kobe cattle. The animals are fed a diet that includes beer and are given daily massages and permitted limited exercise, so that their beef is exceptionally tender. As might be expected, it is also extremely expensive and is sampled in restaurants mainly by inquisitive tourists and by Japanese businessmen with lavish expense accounts.

However, the new food tastes of the ordinary citizen and particularly the young are not being neglected. By 1972, McDonald's was already operating five restaurants in Tokyo, and other American food franchisers were moving rapidly into the capital as well as Osaka and other major cities, anxious to capture their share of the zooming Japanese enthusiasm for the American fast-food hamburger!

Returning to China, here is a more traditional oriental ground meat recipe.

SWEET AND PUNGENT PORK BALLS (China)

1 pound ground lean pork
½ teaspoon onion salt
¼ teaspoon garlic salt
¼ teaspoon ground ginger
2 tablespoons soy sauce
1 egg, beaten
4 tablespoons cornstarch
3 tablespoons peanut oil or salad oil
1 large green pepper, cut in ¾-inch squares
1 7-ounce package frozen Chinese snow pea pods, thawed and well-drained
1 cup very hot water
2 chicken bouillon cubes
¼ cup vinegar
¼ cup sugar
4 slices canned pineapple, each cut into six pieces

In a bowl combine first six ingredients, using only *one tablespoon* of the soy sauce. Add 2 tablespoons of the cornstarch. Blend mixture and shape into about 24 balls, 1 ¼ inches in diameter. Keep palms moistened with cold water to prevent meat sticking to hands. Coat each meat ball lightly with a little extra cornstarch.

Heat 2 tablespoons of the oil in a deep 10-inch skillet. Add pork balls and brown well on all sides. Using a slotted spoon, remove them and set aside in a bowl. Add one more tablespoon of oil to skillet. Add green pepper squares and stir-fry in hot oil for 3 minutes, using a wooden spoon. Add snow pea pods and stir-fry 2 minutes longer. Remove vegetables with slotted spoon and add to pork balls in bowl.

Cool skillet slightly. Add hot water and bouillon cubes. Stir over medium-high heat until cubes dissolve. In a small bowl, combine vinegar, remaining 2 tablespoons cornstarch, sugar, and the remaining tablespoon of soy sauce. Blend smooth and add to liquid in skillet. Cook, stirring, until mixture becomes glossy and thickened. Add pork balls, green pepper, snow pea pods, and pineapple. Heat gently and serve.

Makes 5 to 6 servings. MENU SUGGESTION: serve SWEET AND PUNGENT PORK BALLS with boiled white rice or with Chinese fried rice.

HAMBURGER COOKERY IN THE AMERICAS

LATIN AMERICA Beginning with the year 1492, much of Indian-inhabited America was explored and colonized by Latin peoples of Europe, mainly the Spanish and Portuguese. If Columbus had taken a more northerly route to the New World and landed at Jamestown or Plymouth instead of on an island in the West Indies, the United States itself might have a strongly Latin-influenced culture today.

As it is, the portion of the Americas that did become Latinized is huge. It stretches from Mexico, in North America, to the southern tip of South America and includes Central America and the West Indies.

The Indians occupying this extensive region in pre-Columbian times had arrived there as a Stone Age people. They are believed to have trekked eastward from Asia, probably crossing to America via the land bridge that once existed on the site of the Bering Strait and then wandering south.

During the New Stone Age, these American Indians began to develop as a farming people. Corn was derived from a species of wild grass and adapted to the varied soils and climates—to damp jungle lowlands, temperate grasslands, cool highlands, and even to semi-arid sunbaked plains. Corn, or maize, became the American Indian staple food with few exceptions. In the very cold Andean highlands of Peru and Chile, the potato was developed as a substitute for corn, which would not grow there.

By the time the Spanish conquerors arrived in the New World on the heels of Columbus in the early 1500's, Indian agriculture had contributed to the growth of a widespread Indian population and to several great Indian civilizations, such as the Aztec in Mexico, the Maya in Central America, and the Inca in South America. In their quest for gold, the Europeans almost—but not quite—overlooked the great agricultural wealth of the Indians.

Corn, or maize, was but one of the plant foods that was unknown anywhere else in the world at the time. Also waiting to be discovered by the Europeans were potatoes (both white and sweet) and tomatoes, chili peppers, peanuts, and all sorts of bean and squash varieties, chocolate and vanilla, avocados and pineapples, cassavas and papayas.

Being plant breeders par excellence, the Indians ate a largely vegetarian diet, with beans and peanuts supplying much of their protein. They were not animal herders and so had no regular supply of meat or any milk, butter, or cheese. Turkeys were domesticated in Mexico but not in great numbers. Llamas and alpacas in Peru were used mainly as pack animals and for their wool, and only secondarily for food. Wild animals such as guinea pigs, iguanas, armadillos, wild hogs, and turtles were eaten, and, of course, fish and game birds. But eggs were a rarity. Probably the most reliable source of meat were the special hairless breeds of dogs that the Indians raised for food.

It fell to the Europeans to bring the first cattle, sheep, goats, domesticated pigs, and chickens, as well as wheat, sugar, coffee, and bananas to the New World.

Possibly "dogburger" was the hamburger of the Indians of Latin America before the arrival of Columbus. Today most of the meat that appears in the Latin American cuisine clearly shows European origins, not only in terms of the kind of meat (beef, pork, chicken) but in terms of the cooked dish itself. Yet, because meat of any kind remains a luxury, most Latin Americans, whether pure Indian, *mestizo* (part white, part Indian), West African, or of mixed African, European, and American Indian ancestry, continue to eat low-meat, low-protein subsistence diets based on high-starch corn. For this reason, nearly all of Latin America has been defined as one of the world's major hunger areas.

Yet, in the midst of this "protein desert" are Argentina and Uruguay, each with a predominantly European (Spanish and Italian) population and each with a higher annual per capita meat consumption than that of the United States. Argentina's huge pampas and the fertile grassy plain that covers four-fifths of Uruguay support the great cattle and sheep industries of these countries. Although both countries export much of their beef, mainly to Europe, plenty stays at home for the typical *asado criollo,* a "roast" or barbecue in Creole or native Spanish-American style, at which large slabs of beef are cooked over a pit of smoldering charcoal.

These and other South American countries also have their Spanish-derived meat stews, meat-rich soups, and *empanadas*—small "pies," usually in half-moon shape, stuffed with ground beef (*empanadas de carne*) or other filling. *Picadillo* is another South American hamburger dish, so Spanish-Portuguese in inspiration that its recipe uses olives and raisins and even calls for almonds rather than the Brazil nuts that are native to South America's largest country. *Picadillo,* Spanish for "minced meat" or "hash," is eaten in Cuba and Central America, too. In Portuguese-speaking Brazil, it is known as *picadinho.*

Latin Americans, who cannot afford enough meat for a dish such as this, extend small amounts of chopped or finely diced beef with corn, beans, peppers, squash, and all sorts of other vegetables. Animal parts of cattle, pigs, and sheep, ranging from ears and snouts to trotters and tails are used extensively.

In Mexico and Central America, corn and beef get together in some of the many versions of the *tortilla,* a flat round corncake made from a paste of softened, hulled corn kernels and toasted on a hot ungreased griddle. The *tortilla* is a form of bread as old as this land's Indian civilizations. But its name, meaning "little cake," is Spanish.

A *tortilla* acts as a scoop for the Mexican's everyday dish of boiled black beans seasoned with roasted chili pepper. When fried, dipped in hot sauce, possibly filled with chopped meat or vegetables, cheese or sausage, and rolled up, a *tortilla* becomes an *enchilada*. Folded in half and fried crisp, with a filling inside, it is a *taco*. Fried crisp and flat, with its "filling" piled on top, it becomes a *tostada*. Shredded lettuce and a spicy sauce are almost always added to these *tortilla* variations which can be made to serve as first-rate meat-stretchers.

A cousin to the *tortilla* is the *tamal,* meaning "bundle." *Tamales* are plump little rectangular packages wrapped in cornhusks and steamed. Their insides consist of a layer of corn paste (the same type used in making *tortillas*) topped with a seasoned mixture of chopped beef or chicken, cheese, or other filling. When the *tamal*'s layers of hamburger meat and corn dough are baked in a casserole instead of being steamed in cornhusks, this Indian-Spanish dish of Mexico really becomes an upside down "tamale pie."

EMPANADAS DE CARNE (*Argentina*)

1 tablespoon butter or margarine
1 small onion, finely cut
¼ pound hamburger
⅓ cup grated medium or sharp-flavored Cheddar cheese

3 tablespoons bottled barbecue sauce
salt to taste
1 8-ounce package refrigerated crescent-roll dough

Set oven to 375 degrees Fahrenheit. Melt butter in a 9-inch skillet over medium-high heat. Add finely-cut onion and stir with wooden spoon until light golden-brown. Crumble hamburger over onion, stirring just until meat loses red color. Remove skillet from heat and let cool 10 minutes.

Add grated cheese and barbecue sauce to meat in skillet. Add salt to taste. Divide meat mixture into 8 parts.

Open package of crescent-roll dough. As directed on package, unroll dough and separate into 8 triangles. Spread a portion of meat filling onto each dough triangle. Fold over to form a smaller triangle and seal along edges by pressing down firmly with tines of a fork dipped in flour. Prick top of each filled triangle with fork to allow steam to escape.

Place prepared triangles about 2 inches apart on a lightly buttered baking sheet or other large flat pan with a low rim. Bake at 375 degrees for 10 to 13 minutes or until triangles are golden-brown and puffed. Serve hot.

Makes 4 servings. MENU SUGGESTION: serve EMPA-NADAS DE CARNE at lunch or supper with steaming bowls of bean soup, minestrone, or thick vegetable soup. EMPANADAS also make very good snacks or party food.

PICADINHO (Brazil)

2 tablespoons salad oil or olive oil
2 medium-size onions, cut in very small pieces
1 large green pepper, cut in ¼-inch squares
1 clove garlic, mashed or put through garlic press
1 pound hamburger
1 teaspoon salt
⅛ teaspoon black pepper
¾ cup canned tomatoes, with small amount liquid
¼ cup raisins
¼ cup sliced pimento-stuffed olives
¼ cup sliced almonds

In a deep 10-inch skillet heat oil. Add onion, green pepper, and garlic. Cook over medium heat for 5 minutes, stirring with a wooden spoon.

Crumble hamburger into skillet. Cook just until it loses its red color. Add remaining ingredients except almonds. Cover skillet and simmer over very low heat for 20 minutes.

Add almonds and serve.

Makes 5 to 6 servings. MENU SUGGESTION: serve PICADINHO with rice and a salad of ripe avocado chunks and orange segments in French dressing.

TAMALE PIE (Mexico)

2 tablespoons salad oil
2 medium-size onions, cut in small pieces

1 *clove garlic, mashed or put through garlic press*
1 *small green pepper, cut in ¼-inch squares*
¾ *pound hamburger*
1 ½ *teaspoons salt*
1 ½ *teaspoons chili powder*
2 *cups canned stewed tomatoes, with liquid (1-pound can)*
1 *cup whole-kernel canned corn, well drained (7-ounce can)*
1 *8-ounce or 9-ounce package corn-muffin mix*

In a deep 10-inch skillet heat oil. Add onion, garlic, and green pepper. Cook, stirring, over medium heat until onion is pale golden-brown.

Crumble hamburger into skillet. Cook just until it loses its red color. Add salt, chili powder, tomatoes, and canned corn. Simmer, uncovered, over low heat for 20 minutes, stirring occasionally with wooden spoon.

While hamburger mixture is simmering, set oven to heat to 375 degrees Fahrenheit. Butter a deep 2-quart oven casserole dish. Put corn-muffin mix into a bowl and add ingredients for preparing *cornbread*, as directed on package.

Turn hamburger mixture into casserole. Spoon corn-bread mixture evenly over top. Bake, uncovered, at 375 degrees for 20 minutes or until cornbread is crusty and golden-brown on top. Serve at once, directly from casserole.

Makes 5 to 6 servings. MENU SUGGESTION: serve TAMALE PIE with a crisp apple, raisin, and celery salad in mayonnaise dressing.

THE UNITED STATES   From the jerky of the North American Indian to the fast-food hamburger of the 20th century, meat-eating in the United States has come a very long way. Yet, interestingly enough, both qualify as convenience foods, well-suited to the demands of their day.

Before the coming of the white man, the Indians of the Midwest and the Great Plains were probably the greatest meat eaters in the Americas. The treeless sod of the Plains thundered beneath the hooves of great herds of bison, or American buffalo, and the woodlands of the Rockies and the lesser ranges to the east were full of deer, elk, moose, and bear. Game birds were plentiful, especially in the vicinity of the Great Lakes, which drew masses of waterfowl.

The Plains Indians, in particular, practiced very little agriculture, living largely off the buffalo. Buffalo hunting

was at its peak in late summer and early fall when the animals were at their fattest following a spring and summer of good grazing. The only way the meat from a large kill could be preserved was by drying.

Like Africa's biltong, America's jerky was game meat cut into very thin strips and dried in the sun or sometimes over the heat of a fire. The American Indians jerked buffalo meat and venison. But later, after cattle were introduced, the frontiersmen and scouts prepared jerked beef as well. Tightly wrapped in small packages of dried bark or skin, jerky could be taken on long journeys, for it kept for years. It could be chewed on as was, in leathery strips, or pounded to a powder and cooked into a "stew" with water and cornmeal. The name jerky comes from the Spanish *charqui*, the word used in Latin America to mean meat dried in the sun.

Pemmican was probably the closest thing the North American Indians ever had to hamburger. It was jerked meat pounded into shreds, mixed with dried wild berries and buffalo tallow, and formed into little cakes. It, too, kept for ages, required no cooking, and could be eaten "on the move" like a modern-day highway hamburger.

Once the white man moved onto the Great Plains, first killing off the buffalo, mainly for their hides, and then "busting the sod" for homesteads, the way of life of the Indian buffalo-hunter vanished forever. Also, the consumption of meat, estimated at about 300 pounds per person per year in the game-rich West of the 18th century, began to decline.

With the westward flow of settlers of European background, beef, pork, lamb, and veal came into use as the principal herd-animal meats. Beef was eventually to outstrip all the others. Today Americans eat an average of about 114 pounds of beef a year, about 70 pounds of pork, and only about 4 pounds each of lamb and veal.

In the early days on the Atlantic seaboard, however, the settlers depended mostly on small game, wild birds, and fish for the cooking pot. Even after cattle-keeping was established in New England, beef for the table was something of a rarity in a diet that was based largely on corn and other cereal grains, beans and root vegetables.

The British tradition of stretching a meager meat supply with pastry and piecrust doughs was part of the heritage of the New Englanders and resulted, quite naturally, in the Yankee meat pie. It was made with bits of diced stewing beef (although chopped beef or tiny meat balls came to do just as well) combined with garden vegetables in a beef gravy, and topped with a flour-dough piecrust or with small rolled-and-cut biscuits placed close together with their sides touching. Even nowadays a Yankee meat pie is a tasty and thrifty New England dish, especially when it is prepared with hamburger.

YANKEE MEAT PIE (New England)

1 *cup water*
1 *teaspoon salt*
1 *20-ounce package frozen stew vegetables (potatoes, carrots, onions, celery)*
1 *pound hamburger*
1 *egg, beaten*
3 *tablespoons fine, dried bread crumbs*
½ *teaspoon salt*
½ *teaspoon onion salt*
¼ *teaspoon white pepper*
  flour to coat meat balls
1 *tablespoon butter or margarine*
2 *10-¾ ounce cans beef gravy (2 ½ to 2 ¾ cups)*
1 *8-ounce package refrigerated ready-to-bake biscuits*

In a large (6-cup) saucepan, bring the 1 cup water and 1 teaspoon salt to a boil. Add frozen stew vegetables. When contents begin to boil again, reduce heat and simmer 15 to 20 minutes, or until vegetables are just tender. Pour contents of saucepan into a strainer to drain.

While vegetables are cooking, set oven to heat to 375 degrees Fahrenheit. Combine hamburger and next five ingredients. Roll mixture into balls just under 1 inch in diameter (about 50). Coat meat balls lightly with flour. In a deep 10-inch skillet, melt butter over medium-high heat. Add meat balls and brown on all sides.

Combine meat balls, stew vegetables, and gravy in a deep 2-quart oven casserole dish. Cover dish and bake at 375 degrees for 10 minutes. Remove dish from oven and uncover.

Open biscuit package, separate contents into approximately 10 biscuits, as directed on package, and arrange them on top of mixture in casserole dish, with sides touching. Bake meat pie, uncovered, at 375 degrees for 20 minutes longer or until biscuit topping is puffed and deep golden-brown. Serve at once, splitting the biscuits and spooning some of the gravy from the casserole dish over them.

Makes 5 to 6 servings. MENU SUGGESTION: serve YANKEE MEAT PIE with typical New England accompaniments such as pickled beets and corn relish.

The Midwestern United States, birthplace of the American-style hamburger, continued to be the scene of a plentiful meat supply even after the arrival of the European settlers. Although the habitat of the wild prairie animals was soon converted into farmland, the new "corn belt" served as a granary for the expanding cattle herds, as well as for other domesticated food animals.

The numerous German immigrants to the Midwest had meat-eating traditions of their own that adapted very well to their new homeland. Their old-country recipes

included such dishes as *Hasenpfeffer* ("pickled" rabbit stew), *Sauerbraten* (sweet-and-sour pot roast), and *Schnitzels* (thin-sliced veal cutlets). The Germans were also great sausage-makers, and Hamburg steak had already provided the idea of using chopped fresh beef in various dishes, so baked meat loaf just came naturally to mind. Often, in the Midwest, it was made with several types of ground meat mixed together, such as beef, veal, and pork.

Meat loaf was such a wonderful low-cost meat dish that it became a sort of national institution in the United States, perfect for a hearty family meal. Soon it was being served in all parts of the country, with each cook adding a regional or personal touch to the recipe.

MEAT LOAF *(Midwestern U. S.)*

     1 egg
1 ½ pounds hamburger
    1 cup finely-crumbled day-old white bread (about 2 slices)
    ¼ cup milk
    ½ cup finely grated raw carrot (about 2 carrots)
    3 tablespoons dried onion-soup mix
    3 tablespoons chili sauce
    1 teaspoon salt

Set oven to heat to 350 degrees Fahrenheit. Beat egg in a large mixing bowl. Crumble hamburger over egg and mix well. Add white-bread crumbs. Sprinkle milk over crumbs. Mix thoroughly with meat. Blend in carrot (grated on the fine side of a four-sided grater) and remaining ingredients.

Turn meat mixture into a 9-inch pie plate. Form meat into a mound and smooth its surface. The base of the mound, at the bottom of the pie pan, will measure about 7 ½ inches across. If desired, the meat loaf may be baked in a regular 5x9 loaf pan, but it will have less crusty surface.

Bake meat loaf at 350 degrees for 45 minutes. Remove from oven and let stand in a warm place for 5 minutes before slicing. To serve round meat loaf, cut in pie-shaped wedges.

Makes 6 servings. MENU SUGGESTION: serve MEAT LOAF with baked potatoes, split and topped with chive-seasoned sour cream, and with broccoli with lemon butter. Catsup or chili sauce is a must with the meat.

In the southern United States, the frontier meat animals —bear and deer, squirrel and rabbit, opossum and raccoon, and the peccary or wild pig—gradually gave way to the domesticated hog and the chicken. The southern landscape was not as well suited to cattle-raising as the Midwest and the Great Plains, and the plantation economy, in particular, was favorable to hog-raising. The large estates had smokehouses where hams could be slow-cured for flavor and long-keeping.

Virginia's famous Smithfield hams came from hogs that throve on peanuts, which were planted in large fields tended, like the tobacco and cotton fields, by slaves brought from Africa. The peanut itself was of course native to the Americas.

The South developed a variety of cuisines, marked by special regional dishes. In the coastal lowlands of South Carolina and Georgia, there was a delicate shrimp and rice cookery, while the mountain people of North Carolina and Tennessee favored bolder dishes like home-cured ham with red-eye gravy. Mississippi was "catfish and hush-puppy" country. Of course, fried chicken with cream gravy was eaten just about everywhere in the South, although the "right way" to prepare the South's most famous dish was often fiercely argued.

The Gulf Coast of Louisiana became the home of French and Spanish settlers who intermarried on American soil, creating a segment of the population known as Creole. With the help and the culinary influence of Africans who came as slaves to Louisiana, often by way of the West Indies, a type of cookery also termed Creole came into existence.

Rice was the basis of many Creole dishes such as the thick soup called gumbo, the fish stews that resembled French *bouillabaisse,* and the jambalaya that mixes all

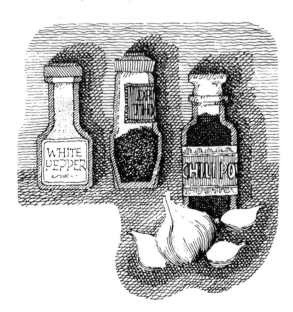

sorts of ingredients—shrimp, ham, sausage, chicken, crabmeat, even oysters—with rice. Jambalaya, which takes its name from the French Provencal word *jambalaia,* means a mixture of diverse elements. Hamburger fits very well into this fine meat-extending dish with its colorful vegetables and its lively Creole seasoning.

JAMBALAYA (Creole U. S.)

1 *cup uncooked rice*
3 *chicken bouillon cubes*
½ *pound bulk pork sausage*
¾ *pound hamburger*
3 *tablespoons butter or margarine*
½ *pound cooked, smoked ham, cut into ¼-inch cubes*
1 *medium-size onion, cut in very small pieces*
1 *medium-size green pepper, cut in ¼-inch squares (about 1 cup)*
1 *large clove garlic, mashed or put through garlic press*
1 *teaspoon salt*
¼ *teaspoon white pepper*
½ *teaspoon chili powder*
½ *teaspoon dried thyme*
1 *28-ounce can tomatoes packed in thick tomato purée (about 3 cups)*

In a large (6-cup) saucepan, cook the rice as directed on the package, adding the chicken bouillon cubes to the water and omitting the salt. While rice is cooking, prepare the following:

Crumble sausage meat into a deep 10-inch skillet and

cook over medium heat, stirring with a wooden spoon, until sausage loses its pink color. Spoon off fat. Crumble hamburger over sausage and continue cooking until meat loses its red color. With a slotted spoon, remove sausage meat and hamburger to a very large bowl. Spoon off fat remaining in skillet. (Let fat solidify before being discarded.) Set oven to heat to 325 degrees Fahrenheit.

Melt 1 tablespoon of the butter in the skillet. Add cubes of ham and toss in hot fat just until lightly browned. Remove and add to bowl with other meats.

Add remaining 2 tablespoons of butter to skillet. Add onion, green pepper, and garlic. Fry on low heat, stirring, until vegetables are pale golden-brown and nearly tender. Add all remaining ingredients. Add contents of skillet to the meats in the large bowl. Add the rice (which should be cooked tender and dry) and mix through gently.

Turn entire mixture into a deep 3-quart to 4-quart oven casserole dish, cover, and heat through at 325 degrees Fahrenheit for 30 minutes or until piping hot.

Makes 8 to 10 servings. MENU SUGGESTION: JAMBALAYA is perfect party fare. Serve with hot, crisp French-bread rolls and a mixed green salad.

It is no surprise that the cookery of the Southwestern United States resembles that of Latin America and particularly of Mexico just across the border. The states of Texas, New Mexico, and Arizona were the scene of early Spanish settlement, developed a Spanish-Indian culture, and actually belonged to Mexico during the first half of the 19th century.

The Indian population of the region shared the agricultural traditions of the Indians of Latin America. They ate little meat aside from small game such as rabbit and the domesticated wild turkey.

The first cattle were longhorns brought from Spain. They were more picturesque than appetizing, for their meat was usually gamy in flavor and tough and stringy in texture. Even after Texas was admitted to the union as a state, in 1845, and began to ship its longhorn cattle to the Midwest, Texan beef was used mainly in the manufacture of the Polish, Italian, and German-style sausages that were well-liked by the immigrant residents of the larger midwestern cities. It was not until shorthorn and Hereford cattle, both of British origin, were brought to the Southwest that the quality of its beef animals improved and the Texas beef barbecue started to become a popular institution.

The word barbecue, today, refers as much to the method of outdoor cooking on a spit or a grill over an open fire or a smoldering pit, as it does to the spicy sauce with which the meat is often brushed or basted. The origin of the Texas barbecue sauce is of course Mexican and, in turn, Indian-Spanish, consisting as it does of tomatoes and chili peppers, garlic and onion, vinegar, oil, spices, and sugar.

Also Spanish-Indian in origin is that most famous of all Mexican-American dishes, *chili con carne,* which probably originated just north of the border where it was considered a good way to utilize the tough beef of the Texas longhorn cattle of the early days.

In this dish, which is now known and very well-liked all over the United States, the *chili* is chili powder, a blend of ground, dried chili peppers, herbs, and spices, and the *carne,* or meat, is none other than our old friend, hamburger. Red beans, sometimes called "chili beans" are the important, meat-stretching ingredient in this dish. If they are not available, red kidney beans, which are slightly larger, may be used instead.

CHILI CON CARNE (Southwestern U. S.)

1 ½ *tablespoons olive oil or salad oil*
  1 *clove garlic, mashed or put through garlic press*
  1 *medium-large onion, cut in very small pieces*
  1 *pound hamburger*
  2 *cups canned tomatoes, with their liquid*
  ½ *6-ounce can tomato paste*
1 ½ *teaspoons chili powder*
  1 *teaspoon salt*
  1 *1-pound can red beans, with their liquid*
  ½ *cup pitted ripe olives*

Heat oil in a deep 10-inch skillet over medium heat. Add garlic and onion and fry just until golden. Crumble hamburger into skillet and cook, stirring with wooden spoon, just until it loses its red color.

Add tomatoes, tomato paste, chili powder, and salt. Cook, uncovered, over medium-low heat for 30 minutes, stirring occasionally.

Add red beans and ripe olives. Continue cooking un-covered, over medium-low heat, for 20 minutes or until most of the liquid has bubbled away and the mixture has thickened. Taste and add more chili powder, if desired. This dish may be made a day ahead, refrigerated, and reheated.

Makes 6 servings. MENU SUGGESTION: serve CHILI CON CARNE with hot corn muffins or cornbread and with a shredded carrot-and-cabbage salad.

Today's hamburger-loving Americans all over the United States often prefer to prepare hamburgers at home, as a change from the machine-stamped products of the fast-food hamburger stand. The home-cooked hamburger offers true economy, better nutrition, greater variety, and the challenge and fulfillment of "doing it yourself." Here are a few recipes for excellent burgers that anyone can prepare in mere minutes.

HAMBURGERS

1 *pound hamburger*
   salt
   dried onion flakes or onion powder
8 *hamburger buns, split*
   soft butter or margarine
   catsup
   pickle slices (if desired)

Shape hamburger meat into eight 2-ounce patties, ¼ inch thick and about 3 ½ inches in diameter.

Sprinkle salt all over the bottom of 9- or 10-inch skillet, or a stove-top hamburger grill, and heat to medium-high. (Salt will prevent hamburgers sticking to pan and will at the same time season them.) Add hamburger patties without crowding them too close together in pan. (Pre-shaped hamburgers taken directly from the freezer may also be cooked this way.) Sprinkle burgers with onion flakes or onion powder. Cook quickly, just until sizzling brown and slightly crusty on bottom. Turn and cook on other side, sprinkling surfaces with additional onion if desired.

While hamburgers are cooking, toast surfaces of split hamburger buns and butter them. Place hamburgers on bottoms of buns, top with catsup and pickle slices, and cover with top halves of buns.

CHEESEBURGERS: After hamburgers have been cooked on one side and turned, top cooked surfaces with thin slices of Cheddar cheese. Let bottoms of burgers brown slightly, then cover skillet partially, leaving a little space for steam to escape. Turn heat very low and continue cooking just until cheese has melted. Proceed as for *Hamburgers.*

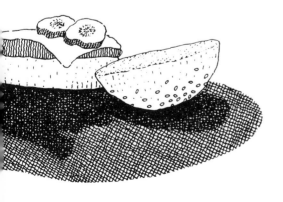

QUARTER-POUND BURGERS

      1 pound hamburger
      3 tablespoons dried onion-soup mix
  1 ½ tablespoons butter or margarine
  1 ½ tablespoons Worcestershire sauce
      4 hamburger buns, split
         soft butter or margarine

Blend hamburger and onion-soup mix thoroughly and shape into four thick patties, about 4 ½ inches in diameter.

In a 10-inch skillet, heat butter and Worcestershire sauce to sizzling. Add hamburgers and fry over medium-high heat until well-browned and slightly crusty on bottom. Turn, lower heat slightly, and cook on other side until browned and of desired doneness in center.

Prepare buns as in recipe for *Hamburgers,* topping burgers with catsup and pickle slices if desired.

FILLED BURGERS: Prepare meat as for *Quarter-Pound Burgers.* Then shape it into eight *very* thin patties, about 4 inches in diameter. In the centers of four of the patties, place about 1 ½ teaspoons of a filling such as shredded Cheddar cheese, crumbled Danish blue cheese, crumbled bacon, pickle relish, fried chopped onion, or crumbled potato chips. Top each with one of the remaining patties and press the edges together tightly so that none of the filling can escape. Cook and serve as directed for *Quarter-Pound Burgers.*

SUPER BURGERS: Cook *Quarter-Pound Burgers* as directed. Before putting between bun halves, top burgers with one or more of the following: Cheddar cheese (melted atop burgers as directed in recipe for *Cheese-burgers*), tomato slices, pickle slices, shredded lettuce, cole slaw, grilled bacon strips, grilled ham slices, French-fried onion rings, and of course catsup, chili sauce, barbecue sauce, mayonnaise, mustard, or any other spread you may like.

The hamburger story has now come full circle, from the very "first" hamburger, eaten raw in a savage landscape four million years ago by a composite ape-man, to the sophisticated grilled hamburger you cooked for your lunch today or bought at your neighborhood fast-food hamburger stand.

What will the future of the hamburger be like? It is intriguing to speculate on the possible trends in ham-burger-eating and hamburger cookery and also on the meat-eating patterns of the world in the coming decades.

For one thing, we can be quite sure that, as the earth's population increasingly outstrips its meat supply, habitual steak-eaters in the "have" countries of the world may find themselves eating more hamburger. Already the United States imports over one billion pounds per year of low-grade beef, to supplement its own supply and to keep pace with the growing demand for meat.

For the "have-not" peoples of the world, the foresee-able future offers little hope that meat will become available as the essential source of protein in their diets. The world's hunger regions—Latin America, Africa, and Asia—now hold nearly three-quarters of the world's population, and unfortunately they are also the regions that are experiencing the most rapid population growth. The United Nations estimates that by the year 2000, 81% of the earth's population will be living in areas customarily stalked by malnutrition, hunger, and famine.

There are a few bright notes, however, in the threatened regions. Since 1955, Japan has managed to stabilize its population growth at around 1 per cent a year, as low or nearly as low as that of most industrial nations of the West. Now China, too, the world's most populous nation with close to 800 million, is aiming for a similar point of stabilization. Already, through a series of massive public-education programs and birth-control campaigns, China's population growth is estimated to have slowed to about 1.8 per cent, well below that of Latin America, Africa, and the rest of Asia, excluding Japan. Perhaps China's example of population planning for fuller use of its own and the world's resources will carry over into some of the other overpopulated and underfed countries of the world.

What about the future of the hamburger on the social and cultural scene?

We can be pretty certain that, as the American-born fast-food industry expands into ever-widening markets, urban Europeans, Asians, and Africans will become more and more like Americans in their addiction to hamburgers.

By early 1973, McDonald's, largest of the U.S. hamburger franchisers, had over 150 restaurants on foreign soil. Among their newest outlets, two had appeared in France, the number of McDonald's restaurants in Japan had exploded to nineteen, forty additional shops were slated for Australia, and a massive McDonald invasion of Great Britain was scheduled for mid-1973. By early 1973, Nairobi, the capital of Kenya, was already sampling the delights of its first Wimpy Bar. Surely other major cities in Africa, South America, and elsewhere would not have long to wait for their first taste of the classic, American-style hamburger-on-a-bun.

It also seems safe to predict that the hamburger future will see more and more Americans learning to cook and enjoy ground-meat dishes of foreign origin at home. Travel, the quest for variety, the increasingly high cost of steaks, chops, roasts, and even stew meat, will put more Swedish and Russian meat balls, more Chinese ground-pork dishes, more Greek and Middle Eastern ground-lamb dishes on American dinner tables.

No longer can hamburger be referred to as "lowly," for the international exchanging of tastes in hamburger may well lead to a more active exchange of cultural ideas among nations, and even—who can say?—to a greater measure of world peace and understanding!

INDEX

CDEFGHIJ—VB—876543279